CHANGING PARTNERS

CHANGING PARTNERS

When Martha Brown, who runs a catering business with her friend Eleanor, discovers her husband, Martin, is 'playing away', she responds in a most unexpected way.

Scenting freedom, she decides that Martin should divorce her and marry Jill. Martin could move in with Jill, say, on Sunday!

However, things don't go according to plan. Martin and Jill fall out and a determined Martha embarks on a series of schemes and stratagems to reunite them, which go disastrously wrong.

All this is put on hold when Martha meets George, an attractive transvestite, Eleanor resigns from Martha's Kitchen at a most inconvenient time and Jill is the only convenient candidate to replace her. Unfortunately, Jill can't cook!

The tangled love lives of the Browns' children, Jeremy and Lucinda, also create problems, in the most unexpected ways, as this delightful carousel of comedy spins to its not-so-inevitable conclusion.

CHANGING PARTNERS

SYLVIA DOWNES

Emissary Publishing
PO Box 33, Bicester, OX26 4ZZ, UK

First published in Great Britain 2009 by Emissary Publishing
PO Box 33, Bicester, OX26 4ZZ, UK.

British Library Cataloguing-in-Publication Data.
A catalogue record for this book is available from the British Library.

ISBN: 978-1-874490-80-7

Cover Design: Mike Rosco

All the characters and situations in this book are purely imaginary
and bear no relation to actual persons

Produced by: Manuscript ReSearch (Book Producers),
P.O. Box 33, Bicester, OX26 4ZZ, U.K.
Tel: 01869 323447
Printed and bound by MWL Print Group Ltd., South Wales.

To my family
who keep me laughing.

ONE

MAY
Friday morning. 11 AM.

Martha mutters to herself: 'List. . .list. . .' as she opens and then closes the fridge door. She's already looked among the many containers – coleslaw, mayonnaise, chilli-sauce – on the work surface. But she missed that piece of paper wedged between the cartons of cream. So that's where she put Jeremy's new mobile number. Still no list though. Now she's getting desperate. She even finds herself looking inside the dishwasher. When the telephone rings Martha is browsing through some packets of nuts on top of the microwave. Where's the phone? Ah, here it is, tucked in among a row of French sticks.

'Hello?'

Martha Brown, an attractive woman in her mid forties, is not looking her best. There are grease stains on her jeans and a smear of something brown and glutinous on her tee-shirt. She has a lot of thick brown curly hair that needs cutting and shaping, a generous figure – that's how she describes it anyway – and good legs and teeth. As she lifts the receiver, she hears a young, nervous, 'have a nice day' – ish kind of voice.

'We want to get married . . .'

'Sorry? Look I really can't stop. Could you ring back? I'm about . . . to go to . . . .'

'Me and Martin.'

'You didn't say your name?'

'Jill, Jill Peters.'

'Do I know him?'

'Who?

'This . . . Martin . . . .'

9

Martha switches off the food processor, which is in the process of massacring a white cabbage.

'Your husband, Martin.'

'Oh that Martin.'

Martha is married. Martha is devoted to her husband and children but quite frankly would prefer to see a good deal less of them.

'Are you still there Mrs Brown?'

Martha has at last found the missing list inside a Delia Smith cookbook. She examines it for a moment and then underlines the word 'salmon' and writes 'to do' beside it. Absent-mindedly she continues to leaf through the book.

Martha Brown cooks for a living and, together with her best friend Eleanor, runs her own catering business: MARTHA'S KITCHEN.

It's just as well that none of Martha's clients can see her kitchen now. Every available surface – and there are a lot of available surfaces in this well designed kitchen – is crowded with containers of food – salads, trifles, quiches, dips . . . .

'Martha, call me Martha. Mrs Brown seems a bit formal in the circumstances. Listen dear. Are you quite sure about this? He's said nothing to me.'

'He doesn't want to hurt you. He's marvellous like that.'

'Like what?'

She marks a place in the recipe book with the list.

'Like . . . well . . . not hurting people. He says there's only one real sin . . . . '

'Only the one? That certainly simplifies things, being able to forget all that nonsense about coveting your neighbour's ass, ox, or . . . .

'So, he doesn't want to hurt me? Bless. Otherwise he'd have come right out with it and said, "Martha. I want to marry Jill Peters".'

'I don't think he would have put it quite like that.'

'No?'

'I don't think he would have said, "Jill Peters".'

'I see what you mean. – "I want to marry Jill. It's bigger than both of us" – is that better?'

'And he's deeply concerned about the children.'

'The children, I see.'

'They being so young?'

'How young?'

Well all three must be under . . . .'

'Three?'

At last Jill has Martha's undivided attention.

12.30.am.

Martha is sitting at the wheel of her car in the local station car park, waiting for her son Jeremy. Drumming her fingers on the wheel she watches a number of people – some carrying cases – enter the car park. It begins to rain. Peering through the wind-screen, Martha spots her son. Fondly she watches a tall fair-haired young man, dressed in a dark blue Parker, denim jeans and carrying a grip, stride athletically towards the car. He climbs in.

'I'm glad you came.'

'You were leaning on me, mum. Might as well try to resist a Force 9 gale.'

Jeremy fastens his seat belt and braces himself against the dash-board as his mother, narrowly missing a green Escort, zooms out of the car park and into a stream of traffic.

'All I said was that Eleanor and I had this wedding reception and our barman and waiter had let us down at the last minute. That can hardly be described as leaning.'

'And, "Jeremy what are you doing this weekend?" in that voice of yours. Mum, the lights have changed!' Closing his eyes, Jeremy says, 'Who is manning the bar?'

'Your father.'

'Not a chance.'

Martha is now driving at speed along the High Street. Ignoring a white van, she turns right, narrowly missing a lorry that is approaching the junction. Jeremy moans softly. Martha ignores him and changes into top.

'Sorry to drag you away from college. Must remember to stop at the wine merchants. How's your flatmate? Is he still going out with that Chinese girl?'

'The girl's Thai and she's dumped him. Anyway Duncan has got other things to worry about now. He's just found out that his dad's a transvestite. His old woman found his old man – are you following me?'

'I'm riveted. I wonder if I've got time to pick up a salmon poacher.'

'. . . dressed in an expensive black number she'd only just bought. Anyway, it looks like Duncan's dad will be moving in with me and Duncan for the time being. You've got a salmon poacher.'

'Your friends lead such interesting lives.'

'My friends can dine out on their families. Not me. My background's so boringly stable. I was born in my own bed for God's sake.'

Jeremy does not know it of course, but all this is about to change.

After completing one or two last minute bits of shopping, Martha finally drives up to the large Victorian semi – gables, large bay windows and porch with pillars – where she and her family live.

There is another car, a Fiat Uno parked in the drive. The car belongs to Eleanor who is Martha's best friend and business partner. As Martha parks beside the Uno she notices the tail end of a fish van disappearing down the road.

'That was the fish van. I expect he's just delivered the salmon.'

Jeremy eyes the Fiat Uno as he climbs thankfully out of his mother's car and reaches into the back seat for his grip.

'You didn't say Eleanor was here.'

'She arrived just as I was leaving for the station and is giving me a hand with all the last minute preparations for tomorrow. Have you remembered all your instructions?'

'I've to collect the glasses and my trousers. . . .'

'And your father's suit from the cleaners. And a salmon poacher. And can you carry the wine into the house for me?'

1.15 p.m.

Eleanor Peters was a model – in a small way – in her twenties. Now, in her early forties, she is still seriously attractive. She is slim and when she moves has the carriage of a dancer. She has streaked blonde hair, which she wears today in a low chignon, cheek bones to die for, almond shaped eyes, full red lips and is wearing hyacinth blue pedal pushers and a paler blue crop top. What is more, she can cook. At present she is filling a meringue case with fruit and cream.

The kitchen is still a hive of activity. The mixer is beating away. The food processor continues to cut and grind. A mound of pastry is waiting on a board to be rolled out. In the absence of her friend, Eleanor has tried to restore some kind of order. She has stacked many of the assorted trays under the work station.

As soon as Martha enters the kitchen, she spots the trays and immediately begins to check through them. Meanwhile Jeremy seizes hold of Eleanor and kisses her.

'Hullo gorgeous.' Martha's friend has a soft spot for Jeremy so she kisses him back. This is a mistake for as she tries to withdraw, he takes an even firmer grip.

'Want a toy boy?'

A bit flustered Eleanor turns to Martha who has completed her inventory now and says, 'The salmon's arrived. And I'm talking salmon here. Not tinned, not in chunks. Eyes, fins, gills, tail.'

Martha switches off the food processor and peers inside.

'Where are they?'

' I've arranged them in the hall.'

'That's my girl,' from Jeremy. Martha frowns for a moment and then her face clears.

'The salmon can defrost in the bath. Jeremy, give El a hand to get them upstairs.'

Jeremy leads the way out of the kitchen, through the dining room and into a long, narrow hall. Little natural light penetrates this part of the house and what there is, is diffused by a stained glass window built into the upper half of the heavy oak front door. Eleanor and Jeremy peer through the aqueous gloom at the glassy eyed salmon, 'swimming' nose to tail, towards the foot of the stairs and then Jeremy picks up a fish in either hand and begins to climb. Eleanor, who can only manage one fish at a time – they are very large and heavy – follows him.

In the kitchen, Martha is multi-tasking. She is making more mayonnaise, dripping oil into the overworked food processor, slicing spring onions, while at the same time shouting – above the noise of the processor – into the mouthpiece of the phone to Jill.

'I'm glad you rang back but . . . .'

'I just had to speak to you again. I wanted to explain, although I knew you would be busy with the children.'

'Yes. . . I. . . .'

'I wanted to thank you for being so understanding and . . .

what's that noise?'

'That's all right. Now . . . .'

'But you must hurt . . . .'

'No'.

'You must.'

'Oh all right. Just a bit.' The mayonnaise has curdled but never mind.

In the bathroom, Jeremy heaves his salmon into the bath, then descends the stairs again. Eleanor places hers in the bath and turns on the cold water tap. Jeremy, returning with two more salmon pauses at the bathroom door to catch his breath.

'Still going strong with what's-his-name?' He lowers the glistening fish into the water.

'Luke? Yes. He wants us to get married.'

'Pity. I'm fancy free at the moment. And I'm looking for somewhere else to live. It will be a bit crowded now Duncan's dad's moved in.'

Jeremy makes one more trip down to the hall to retrieve the last salmon. Eleanor contemplates the glassy-eyed fish for a few moments and then turns on the hot water tap. He returns.

'And I go for older women. Especially beautiful, sexy blondes like my mum's best friend.'

Eleanor smiles and then says slowly: 'Well I'll bear that in mind.'

Friday evening. 5.45 p.m.

Martha and Eleanor are both in Martha's kitchen. Martha is talking on the phone to Jill yet again while Eleanor noisily stacks the dish washer. Eleanor is annoyed and with good reason. Martha hasn't got time to be talking on the phone.

'It's been lovely talking to you but I must bath Lionel.'

'Jeremy's the baby isn't he?'

'The youngest . . . certainly . . . .'

'So you don't mind my seeing Martin tonight?'

'Not at all. Keep him as long as you like. I've got lots to do here. Bye.'

Eleanor crams more plates into the dish washer and then moves over to the oven from which she removes two quiches. Martha pulls up a chair to the kitchen table, reaches behind her, opens the fridge door and takes out a bottle of wine. She pours herself a glass and gestures with the bottle to Eleanor, who shakes her head.

'No thanks. I haven't got time. Neither have you. The salmon needs poaching for a start. Martha, what's going on? You've been on that phone off and on all day.'

Taking her time about it, Martha sips her wine and finally says:

'I have been chatting to a friend of Martin's. His . . . how shall I put it? – bit on the side.'

Eleanor sits down at the table and reaches for the bottle. Martha grins evilly.

'I thought that would give you pause for thought. It's given me pause for thought I can tell you.'

Eleanor is not at all sure what the appropriate response to this piece of information is so she opts for silence. Martha, glancing sideways at her friend, continues reflectively:

'Who'd have thought he had it in him?'

Eleanor risks: 'How do you feel about it?'

Martha considers for a moment and then says, 'Pleased on the whole.'

Eleanor processes this information and then:

'You were talking about bathing Lionel and a baby Jeremy. What's all that about?'

'It's very simple. My dear husband has been lying about his age. He's told this girl that he has three children all under five. I'm playing along with it for the moment.'

'I see,' says Eleanor slowly, though she doesn't. 'How old is she?'

'Twenty-four and she's his secretary.'

Eleanor laughs. 'Well that's original. Twenty-four? A year older than your Lucinda.'

Has she got her own flat?'

'Yes. He could move in on Sunday.'

Eleanor is not sure if Martha is as cool about all this as she appears but knowing her friend, she's prepared to give her the benefit of the doubt. So she says lightly:

'All being well.' Then warming to this intriguing situation she asks, 'Martha, how are you going to play it? What if he wants to keep the arrangements as they are?'

'He's well set up isn't he? An adoring young mistress and . . .'

'. . . a cynical sharp tongued wife . . .'

'who is clever and can cook . . . .'

Eleanor goes to the fridge and takes out another bottle of wine as Martha makes her position clear: 'I have no intention of leaving things as they are. Martin has found himself a young mistress so the best thing all round is if he divorces me and marries her.'

Eleanor opens the bottle of wine and pours herself another glass.

'Just like that. Come on, Martha, after all these years? I thought you loved Martin in your fashion. I know you've been droning on for ages about being bored, wanting your freedom, but I thought that was all talk.'

'I do love him – in my own way – but that doesn't mean I want to live with him. In fact I'm fed up with living with him. We've been married for too long. I've told you. I've read the book . . .'

'I know – seen the video, bought the tee-shirt.'

Eleanor goes to the fridge, riffles inside for a moment or two and then emerges with half a quiche. She cuts herself a slice, then finds a plate and loads it with quiche, half a tomato, two pickled onions, three gherkins, a slice of ham and a slab of cheese. Returning to the table with her loot she says through a mouthful of food: 'And here am I considering taking the plunge.'

Martha tries to help herself to one of the gherkins, but Eleanor pushes her hand away.

'Don't do it El. You can't seriously be considering marrying a man called Luke. He plays the recorder for god's sake.'

'What's wrong with the recorder?'

'Nothing for a ten year old. I used to play. I was rather good as a matter of fact.'

'I remember.'

You don't have to marry him, El. If you do, you'll be ironing his shirts and washing his socks before you've finished eating the wedding cake.'

'I love him Martha.'

'Take my advice. If you want the candle-lit dinners to continue, stay single.'

'If only. Luke isn't the candle-lit dinner type. Sardine sarnies are more his style.'

Eleanor has polished off all the food on her plate now. She gets up again and begins to lift various trays and cartons.

Martha watches her with growing irritation and finally says, 'What are you looking for?'

'The biscuit tin.'

'Behind those French sticks, but I expect it's empty. Jeremy's home, remember.'

Eleanor locates the biscuit tin and, after a bit of excavation, finds a couple of ginger nuts, which she proceeds to eat.

'Anyway we were talking about you and Martin, not me and Luke. Always assuming you can persuade Martin to move in with this Jill, would you consider marrying again?'

'I don't believe you just said that Eleanor. Me remarry? Never. Been there. Done that. Read the book. Seen the video. Got the tee-shirt.'

'You could be lonely.'

'I'll risk it.'

'What about sex?'

'I shall have a series of affairs – no strings attached. I've never had an affair you know. I reckon it's about time I started.'

'Affairs are not all they're cracked up to be and I should know.'

The two women relapse into a comfortable silence for moment or two and then Eleanor, who is gradually adjusting to the fact that her best friend and her husband might split up, says slowly, 'I don't believe you've thought this thing through, Martha. For instance, now you know about Martin's affair, how are you going to play it? Cool or the injured wife? I think he would prefer the injured wife. He'd feel more secure with the injured wife.'

'I'll play it by ear. I usually do.'

'I wish you wouldn't cook by ear. What did you put into the salmon marinade? I hope you didn't get mixed up between cayenne and paprika again.'

Martha gets up from the table.

'The salmon. Yes we've got to get started on the salmon.'

'Have you seen the size of them?'

'Of course. There's one simmering away in the poacher as I speak. Have faith. The main problem is where to put them, when they're cooked. The fridge is full. And the freezers?'

She looks round the room, seeking inspiration. ' I know. When they are wrapped in their foil cosies we'll store them in the cupboard in the dining room. Remind me to load the salmon before we set off for the reception.'

Martha goes to the stove and lifts the lid of the salmon poacher.

' I wonder if she's told him yet.'

'Told him what?'

'That I know.'

TWO

Friday/ midnight

Very drunk, Jeremy is lurching down a street of up-market terrace houses. He does a twirl round a lamp-post and then, after stationing himself outside the door leading to Eleanor's flat, begins to sing 'The Street Where You Live' from 'My Fair Lady'. Surprisingly, for one who prides himself on being a cool hip-hop fan, Jeremy is also a passionate lover of musicals. His passion – and we're talking Oklahoma, Kismet, The King and I, here, not Chicago, Blood Brothers or The Entertainers – began when he was in the sixth form and got to play Freddy in My Fair Lady. Jeremy has a pleasant tenor voice and, when sober, sings well in tune. Unfortunately tonight he is far from sober. Six pints of Abbots Ale have affected his sense of pitch. Anyway he is well into the second chorus when Eleanor's car draws up. Almost beside herself with rage – she can see that old busybody's curtains across the way, twitching – she gets out of the car.

'Jeremy!'

He continues to warble: 'But the pavement always stayed beneath my feet before.'

'Jeremy!'

She grabs his arm.

'Shut up, Jeremy. You're disturbing the neighbours. Come on!'

Still keeping a firm grip, she hustles the young man towards the door of the house and puts her key in the lock. To Eleanor's relief, he has stopped singing now but, almost equally infuriating, he has started to giggle.

'SHHH! Mush be quart SSHHH!' He chortles.

Eleanor pushes him into a narrow hallway, where he crashes into a small table. She rights the table and then attempts to propel him towards the flight of steps that leads to her flat but he collapses on the first step. Eleanor is a determined woman. She drags her friend's son to his feet and supports him up the stairs. On the way up the young man, having abandoned music, now turns to verse:

'She walks in Beauty . . . like the . . . like the . . . .'

'You're seriously getting on my nerves Jeremy. Shut up! Move!'

Jeremy staggers up four more steps and then sits down heavily again.

'Get up. Now.' He gazes soulfully up at his mother's friend. She looks entrancing, although somewhat blurred. Her hair has fallen in loose curls onto the shoulders of the long dark blue duster coat she is wearing.

'We spend a lot of time on stairs you and me El. We have what you might call a 'staircase relationship.''

He begins to sing again.

'All at once am I seven stories high . . . .'

'Come on. Please Jeremy!'

Eleanor nearly gives up at this point, but as I say she is a determined woman so, after a further struggle, she manages to get the young man up the stairs and through the door of her flat. She propels him into her kitchen. It is a tiny oak-veneered galley with a table and two chairs set in the centre. Eleanor manhandles Jeremy into one of the chairs. He is unable to maintain an upright position, however. He falls forward, his head resting on the table.

Muttering to herself, Eleanor begins to prepare coffee. She fills the kettle then slams open a cupboard door to find a tin. Roused from his torpor by all this noise, Jeremy looks up blearily and says, 'El? Watcher doin' El?'

'I'm making you some coffee.' The kettle boils as she does this and Jeremy falls to the floor.

'Eleanor! Look, I'm on my knees.'

'So you are.' Eleanor opens her bag, takes out a comb and proceeds to gather her hair into a pony tail. She refuses to look at her friend's son who, at this point will do just about anything to gain her attention.

'Fairest Helen. Be mine. Marry me.'

'OK,' without looking at him.

'What?'

'I said okay. Drink your coffee and then I'll ring for a taxi. We're engaged.'

Saturday morning 1 a.m.

The night is far from over although Martha Brown, exhausted after her day's exertions, is tucked up in bed, fast asleep now. Martin, Martha's husband is not lying beside his wife though. He is sinking into a post coital doze next to his mistress. Jill is very pretty in a Dresden doll sort of way with a shining cap of golden hair, the milky skin that goes with a true blonde, and a slim shapely figure. Has this paragon no physical defects? When Martha finally comes to meet the girl, she notes that Jill's ankles are on the thick side and that her China blue eyes are set too close together, but then Martha might be prejudiced.

Martin's head rests on a white lace-edged pillow that matches the white lace-edged duvet that has slid to the floor and the white lacy curtains that hang at the bedroom windows. Martha's husband might be nodding off to sleep but Jill's large blue eyes are wide open and this is because she is trying to get up the nerve to make a confession. Finally she takes a deep breath and begins:

'Pooh Bear.'

'Yes, Piglet?'

'I've got something to tell you, Pooh, but Piglet is scared Pooh might be cwoss.

'You're sounding a bit Eeyor-ish Piglet.'

'I feel a bit Eeyor-ish Pooh.'

'Tell Pooh all about it.'

'You'll be cwoss Pooh.'

Martin tries to sit up, but Jill plants her head firmly on his chest, so he falls back onto the pillows again.

'Come on Piglet. Out with it. Pooh Bear has to go back to his den soon.'

'Don't go Pooh. Piglet will cwy if Pooh goes back to his den.'

'Pooh has to go. Pooh has to make sure all his little bear cubs are safe.'

Martin gently lifts Jill from his chest and sits up. Then, to her dismay, he gets out of bed and begins to search for his scattered clothes.

'Pooh doesn't love Piglet any more. Pooh didn't eat the dinner Piglet cooked.'

Martin laughs indulgently as he buttons up his shirt.

'Now that's not true Piglet. I could get quite fond of burnt spaghetti given time.' Jill pouts prettily but Martin is not looking.

'You distracted me Pooh, when I was cooking. Distract me again. I like being distracted.'

He is scrabbling under the bed searching for his tie now.

'I'd love to stay and distract you again darling, but I really must go. Jeremy's teething. It's just not fair. I wish I was the kind of chap who could switch off his responsibilities but I'm not.'

He has located his tie but is now having difficulty finding his trousers.

Jill takes a deep breath and then says in a rush, 'She told me to keep you here as long as I liked.'

Martin continues the trouser search and starts scrabbling about on a trunk that sits beneath the bedroom window. He finds a pink rabbit, a white panda, two rag dolls and his trousers.

24

'Where's my shoes?'

'Try under the dresser. No, let me.'

Jill gets out of bed and then crawls towards a frilly dresser in search of the shoes but is unable to find them. She looks up just in time to see Martin trip over the trailing duvet and fall full length beside the bed.

'I've broken my toe. Shit.'

He hops about for a bit before landing heavily back onto the bed. Unfortunately, he puts out a hand to support his weight as he descends towards the bed. This is a mistake.

'I've broken my wrist.'

Martin falls onto his back moaning softly. Jill joins him on the bed and pauses to kiss him between each sentence.

'Poor Pooh bear . . . . Did he hurt his toe then? . . . And bump his head? . . . And his paw? . . . Is that better? I must kiss it all better. . . . Let me distract you.'

Martin allows himself to be coaxed back onto the bed, kissed and comforted. His brain hasn't entirely disengaged, however. Suddenly remembering Jill's earlier remark, he mumbles, 'What did you say?'

'Mm?'

'What did you say . . . before . . . .'

'I don't rem . . . ember.' She is working her way down his body now.

'You said, "She told me".'

Jill sits up. 'That's right. So you can get undressed again and get back into bed.'

'Who's she?'

'Martha.'

'Martha? Martha who?'

'Your wife, Martha. We had a nice ch . . . '

'Martha?' Martin's normally deep voice has risen an octave.

'She seemed nice.'

'Nice?' the voice scales another octave.

'Very nice. We became good friends.'

'Friends!' Martin's face has turned an unattractive puce colour.

'I wish you wouldn't keep repeating everything I say. It makes me nervous.'

'Nervous!'

'There you go again.'

'Just explain. Slowly, clearly, so I can get it straight. Are you trying to tell me that you have been to see my wife?'

'Oh no. I wouldn't do that darling; not without telling you first. I rang her up.'

'When? When did you ring my wife?'

'This morning at about eleven. You had that appointment with the nice Mr. . . .'

'Why did you ring her?'

'To tell her about us. I thought it for the best. You said this was all tearing you apart. It's tearing me apart too, darling, so I told her everything. She was very sympathetic. She wasn't at all as I expected. She was very brave.'

'What did she say? What did she say? Christ! I just can't believe you've done this.'

Martin has leapt off the bed now and is pacing up and down. While on his travels he spots one of his missing shoes by the window. He sits down on the bed and crams one foot into it.

'Why are you so cross? Martha wasn't cross. She was very calm. Positively Kangor-ish in fact.'

Martin leaps from the bed and begins to crash about the room, looking for the other shoe. He finds it by the door, sits down on the bed again and puts it on. Jill gathers up the duvet, drapes it round her shoulders and sits up in bed watching him.

'I've gotter go! I've gotter go! Where's my fuckin' socks?'

'Why have you got to go Martin? Martha doesn't mind

you being here. She said so. Martin!'

Martin finds his socks tangled up at the bottom of the bed. He takes off his shoes, puts on his socks and then replaces the shoes.

'I don't believe this is happening. I'll wake up in a minute. Where's my fuckin' coat?'

Jill gets out of bed, finds the coat draped over a chair and hands it to him.

'Well when you get home make sure that little Jeremy is all right. I think he got a bit wet today. Martha was telling me he . . . .'

'Little Jeremy?' Martin is struggling into his coat now.

'Martha said . . . .'

'I wish you'd stop calling her Martha in that revoltingly chummy way.'

'We are chums. Great chums. She told me to call her Martha. She said Mrs Brown was a bit formal in the circumstances.'

Saturday morning   2 a.m.

Blithely unaware of all this, Martha is curled up on the left side of hers and Martin's double bed. It is set dead centre of the large untidy room that is their bedroom. There are two low tables, one piled high with books, either side of the bed with a lamp on each table. Opposite the bed is a row of fitted cupboards. The cupboard doors are open, revealing a set of drawers to the left and serried ranks of clothes to the right. There is also a large dressing table, scattered with make-up, odd pieces of jewellery, combs and brushes.

Martha does not stir when Martin, moving cautiously, enters the room. He takes off his trousers and then sits down on his side of the bed to remove his shoes. Once undressed he puts on his pyjamas all the time casting anxious glances in the direction of his sleeping wife. Finally he climbs into bed, lies still for a moment and then gently touches her back.

'I say. Are you asleep? Mar . . . .'

Startled, Martha half sits up, groans and then lies down again.

'Sorry. I didn't mean to wake you. I wasn't expecting you to be asleep.'

'What time is it for God's sake?'

'Five past two.' Then, after a pause: 'Martha I can smell fish. The bathroom reeks of it.'

Martha sits up properly now.

'Five past two and you weren't expecting me to be asleep?' She lies down again, murmuring, 'Fish?'

'In the circumstances. I wasn't expecting you to be asleep in the circumstances.'

Martha mutters over her shoulder, 'What circumstances? Is there a fire?' Then sits up again.

'Is Jeremy all right? Lucin . . . ?' At this point the memory tapes reactivate and she says sarcastically, 'Sorry to disappoint you, Martin, but I was asleep and I intend to go back to sleep right now.'

She snuggles down into bed and then murmurs as she sinks into her pillow. 'You could check if Jeremy's in. And make sure he has locked the door.'

'He's in the kitchen . . . sort of moaning to himself.'

'I hope he's not ill. He needs to work, what with finals coming up next year.'

'Darling, we have to talk.'

Martha turns onto her back and opens her eyes reluctantly.

'All I want is a chance to explain.

'Not now, Martin. You know I need my sleep. So should you if you've been on the job.' Martin looks pained but is distracted almost immediately.

'Fish, Martha! I can still smell it. I smelt it as soon as I walked into the house.'

Martha does not wish to go into an explanation of where she defrosted the salmon right now so she says:

'Anyway, there's nothing to explain. Your friend explained the whole thing very clearly. You want to marry her and divorce me.' She yawns. 'Seems straight- forward enough to me. It's not rocket science or anything. Let me set your mind at rest. You can have your divorce on one condition: you act as my barman tomorrow. Luke can't do it.'

'Luke who?'

'You know Luke, Eleanor's boyfriend. Anyway he can't do the wedding reception.'

'All right, all right, I'll do it. Now, darling . . . .'

'I thought you might and will you please stop calling me 'darling'. You never call me darling. It makes me nervous.'

She turns over in bed. 'Can I go to sleep now?' And yawns again. Unfortunately, Martin, who has lived with his wife for years and therefore should know better, can't let the matter drop. Eleanor's right. Martin would have felt more comfortable with an injured wife.

'Stop pretending, dar . . . Martha. I know you must be feeling hurt and . . . .'

'Martin, don't tell me what I'm feeling. I know what I'm feeling. I'm feeling tired.'

Martha warms to her theme. 'It's been a busy day and tomorrow will be even busier. I've cooked, sorted out crockery, glasses, plates; I collected Jeremy from the station. Then there was the long saga from your friend. And all those bloody salmon.'

Martha is too tired to sustain the indignation long though and soon, sinking down into her pillow she begins to drift off to sleep, muttering: 'Life's at a low ebb at this time of night.

Well known fac . . . .'

She sleeps. Here Martin makes a really serious mistake. He prods his wife in the back again and says: 'Martha, Martha, . . . darling . . . I won't be able to sleep until we've sorted all this out. I just want to tell you . . . .'

The trouble is that Martin, who runs his own software company and is in fact quite bright, lacks what I believe is called emotional intelligence. Therefore he is unable to grasp that this is not the right time to talk things through.

All Martha knows, though, is that her clod of a husband has awakened her yet again. This is a prod too far. She shoots up in bed and bellows.

'I don't care whether you sleep or not. All I know is that I am fuckin' well going to.'

Martin tries to take his wife into his arms, which proves not to be a good move. 'You are angry. I don't blame you. I've behaved disgracefully, let me explain . . . .'

Martha will have none of it. She thrusts him away and cries, 'If I'm angry it's because I can't sleep. I'm tired. How many times do I have to tell you? Now if you can't be quiet go and sleep in Lucinda's room.'

Martha pauses at this point and remembers a piece of information that will wipe that smug expression from her husband's face.

'Lucinda rang just as I was coming to bed. She's moved in with that chap . . . old enough to be her father . . . French Horn player . . . what's his name? Manfred.'

'She's what?'

'I told her you wouldn't be pleased.' She yawns. Martin tries again to put an arm round his wife: 'Martha.'

'Don't tell me. I don't want to know. If you can't sleep, just lie awake quietly. That's all I ask.'

Martha sleeps and Martin lies awake beside her. Quietly.

THREE

Saturday morning 9 a.m.

Martha's kitchen has been restored to some kind of order, but every available space is filled with trays of food, boxes of crockery, glasses and wine waiting to be loaded into cars. Martha, wearing a smart aubergine suit and black heels, is peering into the fridge looking for a carton of double cream because she has discovered a trifle minus the topping.

'Cream . . . cream . . . Where's the . . . ah!'

She switches on the food processor and empties the cream into it. As she does so Martin enters the kitchen wearing baggy pyjama bottoms and a sagging beige sweatshirt. He does not look good, partly because he cut himself while shaving – three bits of toilet paper cover the cuts – and partly because his skin has an unhealthy greyish tinge. The great purple blotches beneath his eyes don't help either.

He mutters, 'Can you turn that thing off.'

Martha shouts above the noise of the food processor, 'If you want toast, the toaster is . . . is . . . under those trays and the bread . . . oh sod it . . . I used the last half loaf for bread crumbs.'

Martin, trying to shift a box manages to knock over a pile of quiches.

'No! Don't move that! Or that!' she shouts, as he tries to find the kettle. 'Look why don't you have some cornflakes?'

'I don't want anything.'

Martha switches off the processor, removes the cream and begins to fold it over a trifle. Sighing heavily, Martin takes a box of plates from a chair and sits down.

'We have to talk.'

'Talk? Talk? What's that? We don't talk. All we ever do is exchange information.'

She's finished the topping and now starts checking – for

the tenth time – the prepared cartons and boxes against a list.

'Well I want to talk now.'

'Oh well in that case I'll ring the bride and say the reception is off. I'll tell her mother to nip out and buy 300 packets of crisps and some nuts. My husband has suddenly decided that he wants a chat, I'll explain. Martin, take your elbow out of that gateau.'

'Christ!' He removes his elbow from a tray of cakes and looks up to see his wife opening the kitchen door. She picks up a stack of cartons and prepares to carry them out to the waiting car. Martin watches his wife in a kind of bemused despair.

'Now where are you going?'

'I thought I might take a stroll.'

She exits the kitchen by a door that leads directly onto the drive, where her estate car is parked. The back seats have been pushed down to make more space. The boot is open.

Martha begins to load the boot. She moves backwards and forwards between the kitchen and the car carrying packages, boxes, crates of wine/whatever. Martha packs efficiently and system-atically, rearranging and repacking where necessary to maximise the available space. After watching his wife carry out the first load, Martin rouses himself to help her. The two soon establish a system. Martin carries out the boxes and trays to his wife and she arranges them in the boot. As they work Martin tries to plead his cause.

'I know things look bad at the moment but I want you to know that I do love you, Martha.'

'Bring the box of wine next. Sod it!' she curses as she traps her hand under the jack.

She shifts the jack to make more room.

'I love you, Martha and I always will.'

'Well that's all right then,' she responds, vaguely.

'I don't want to lose you . . . or the children.'

'Our sweet little boys.'

'I've been foolish I know but men sometimes do . . . .'

'Or the house.'

'What?'

'You wouldn't want to lose the house.'

'I don't care about the house.'

'Don't you Martin? Has Jill got a nice flat?'

'It's all right. It's in Grantley Avenue.'

Martha is impressed. 'Then it must be quite swish.'

'Her aunt left it to her.'

'Well that's a weight off my mind. I wouldn't have wanted you moving into some pokey bed-sit.'

'I'm not moving anywhere. I want things to go on just as before.'

'I bet you do.'

'I'll give her up. It won't be easy, but for the sake of our marriage, I'll do it. It will break the poor kid's heart. She adores me.'

'She does. You must be out of your mind even to consider giving her up. Giving up a lovely, young . . . she is lovely, isn't she?'

'Ravishing.'

'. . . girl who loves you, for a middle aged woman who. . . .'

'Martha . . . .'

'. . . with a flat.'

'It's not fair on you. You've given up the best . . . .'

'There.' Martha makes a final adjustment to the boot while Martin makes another sortie into the kitchen and returns with a single box. Martha places it on top of a pile of other boxes and closes the boot.

'There's more trays by the kitchen table.'

'El will have to take them.'

They both return to the kitchen, which appears larger now that all the food and gear for the wedding has been removed. Martin slumps down onto his chair by the empty table. Martha fills the kettle on and puts out two mugs.

'I don't want a divorce Martha.' And he doesn't. Martin has lain awake all night thinking about the whole situation and he's come to the conclusion, that much as he's enjoyed his relationship with Jill, he is not prepared to sacrifice his marriage for it. He likes his home and Martha's cooking. He does not want to live in Jill's flat. He does not want his children to know about his affair and the lies he has told. Suddenly he feels embarrassed about the whole thing.

His aim therefore, is to re-establish himself in Martha's good books. What he fails to understand is that although he has decided that he wants to remain married to Martha, she has no intention of remaining married to him. Needless to say, Martha can read her husband like a book and is rather enjoying watching him suffer. She says in a sweetly reasonable voice, but with an edge, 'Martin, you are not thinking straight this morning. That's because you are in a state of shock. When you've thought everything through properly, you will be delighted that I am making it all so easy for you both. You will come to realise that Jill is just what you need right now. Imagine coming home each night and sitting down to dinner with a lovely young wife.'

'She can't cook.'

'You can teach her. You're quite a good cook. You like cooking.'

'I'm never allowed near the stove.'

'There you are then. Jill will allow you near her stove. You cook. She can stack the dish-washer.'

'She hasn't got a dish-washer.'

Martha is getting desperate: 'I'll throw in the dish-washer.'

Martin looks at his wife in amazement. 'I can't make you out.'

For one moment, Martha is overcome by a great wave of desolation. Mentally she gives herself a shake. This is what she wants isn't it? Before she can analyse her emotions the desolation is replaced by resentment and she says sharply, 'No. You never could. You don't know me very well.'

'Know you? Don't be ridiculous. We've been married for twenty-five years.'

Suddenly she feels on firmer grounds. This is a game that she is good at. 'What's my favourite colour?'

'Now you are being silly.'

'I stopped taking sugar in my tea, three years ago, and it still hasn't sunk in.'

'Oh for god's sake.'

'What do I think about: Green Peace; Buddhism; The Cinema Today; Human Rights, the state of the ozone layer; September 11th; the Middle East; the war in Iraq, global warming?'

'Martha!'

'Boiling lobsters alive . . . .'

'Martha! Christ! You 're impossible.'

The resentment and anger fade. Martha is enjoying herself again.

'I am, I am! Jill wouldn't go on like that, would she? I don't know how you've put up with me all these years.'

There is a long pause. Martha collects the coffee cups and rinses them in the sink.

Martin is still trying desperately to come to terms with his wife's attitude. Why is she behaving like this? The woman's irrational and that's the truth. Then suddenly a dreadful thought strikes. 'Is there someone else?'

Martha turns to gaze at her husband.

'Now who's being ridiculous? When would I have time to have an affair? I'm an intelligent woman. I've got more sense than to saddle myself with another man, especially now . . . when there's a chance I might get rid of . . . .'

Martha realises that she has gone too far when she sees her husband stiffen.

Fortunately, two simultaneous events distract Martin's attention at this point. Eleanor, dressed in a cream trouser suit, her hair arranged into a severe French pleat arrives at the same time as Jeremy opens his bedroom door and releases a burst of loud pop music. Jeremy calls down from the landing:

'Where's the clothes brush?'

In a voice that can be heard three streets away Martha replies, 'In the airing cupboard.'

Wincing slightly, Eleanor sits down opposite Martin at the kitchen table and looks expectantly from husband to wife. When neither of them speaks, she says jauntily:

'Morning Eleanor. How are you Eleanor? I'm fine, thank you, but I think we should be . . . .' She pauses and when there is still no response she asks,

'What's going on?' Then thinks better of it. 'No, don't tell me. Martha, we must be off.' At last Martha finds her voice. Self consciously she clears her throat and says in an artificially chatty voice, 'Martin's been telling me all about his new friend, Jill. He and Jill are thinking of getting married. When our divorce comes through that is. Did I mention that Martin and I were getting a divorce?'

'Did you?' Eleanor is confused. How much is she supposed to know?

'No, I didn't. What do you think? Martin and I would really value your opinion.'

'About what?'

'About the divorce, me and Martin's divorce. You're a bit slow this morning.'

Jeremy shuffles into the kitchen at this point and despite the fact that he's wearing smart black trousers, a crisp white shirt and a dinner jacket, he looks terrible. His eyes are bloodshot, his face is drawn, his skin doughy; his shoulders are slumped. Jeremy has aged over night.

In a subdued voice, not meeting her eye, he mutters, 'Hi

Eleanor.' Eleanor rises to her feet and kisses him soundly.

'Good morning, darling.'

Martha looks at her son anxiously, 'You do look a bit pale. Are you all right?' She picks a few white hairs off his dinner jacket.

'He looks gorgeous. What a hunk.' Eleanor finds another hair and smoothes the jacket across her fiancé's shoulders.'

Jeremy, looking hopelessly from one woman to the other, finally says tonelessly, 'I need a clothes brush. The cat slept on my jacket. I can't wear it like this.'

Eleanor fumbles in her bag and producers a pocket clothes brush. 'I've got one here. Let me.' And makes a big production of brushing him down. Jeremy is seriously embarrassed but has no choice but to submit.

Meanwhile Martha is assembling the remaining food that Eleanor is to take.

'Pass that tray Martin. This lot will go in your car won't it El?'

But Eleanor hasn't finished tormenting Jeremy yet. She reaches up and undoes his bow tie. 'There. Let me do this, sweetie.' She kisses him. 'Now doesn't he look wonderful? I could stuff and frame him.'

Martha looks at her watch in horror. 'Martin, go upstairs and change right now.'

Eleanor starts to pick up her load, but there is too much for her to carry.

'I can't manage it all. Tell you what. I'll take Jeremy with me. He can give me a hand to unload the other end.'

'Good idea,' Martha says, to Jeremy's despair. He reluctantly picks up the remaining tray.

As she leaves, Eleanor says, 'Don't forget the salmon, Martha. See you there.'

Jeremy tries one last desperate: 'I haven't had any . . . .' But Eleanor propels him through the door.

Martha turns to look down at her husband, who is still slumped in his chair.

'Cheer up, you are a lucky man. Jill sounds lovely.'

Martin brightens a little at the thought of his secretary. 'She is. She's a natural blonde with big blue eyes that have these darling little crinkles at the corners when she laughs.'

This is not what Martha wants to hear. She says caustically, 'Tell me about her wrinkly eyes upstairs.'

Martin is alarmed. What has his wife got in mind? 'Upstairs?'

Martha knows exactly what he is thinking and has half a mind to demand instant sex when she gets him into their bedroom. But there isn't time. So she says instead. 'While you are changing.'

As they mount the stairs Martin says anxiously, 'I didn't say wrinkly, I said . . . . '

FOUR

Saturday. Midday

The wedding reception is about to start. The wedding guests are milling about the foyer of the Crown Hotel. They are a smart looking crowd for this is a smart white tie and tails wedding. The Master of Ceremonies, a large, imposing man with a red face and bulging waistcoat is standing beside the bride, groom and best man, explaining that in a few minutes they should lead the way into the dining room. The guests have other plans though. Most of them are making for the bar – dark oak, brass fittings, hunting pictures – where Martin, dressed in a dinner jacket and bow tie is waiting. A short, stout, balding man in a light weight beige suit that is bursting at the seams, is the first to order. He is accompanied by an aristocratic looking tall blonde, who perches herself on a bar stool.

'A gin and tonic, half a lager and a white wine please.'

'Dry or sweet sir?'

'Dry or sweet, Samantha?

'Dry, darling, and some peanuts.'

Martin pours out the drinks and hands out the peanuts.

'And the gin and tonic . . . and peanuts, sir.'

More guests flock into the bar and Martin is so busy serving them, that he fails to notice Jill threading her way through the crowds towards him. She is dressed in a short, clinging, pink dress that leaves her arms and a good deal of her shoulders bare. She seats herself on the bar stool next to Samantha.

'Dry white wine plea . . . Martin!'

Martin looks at her in consternation. 'Jill!'

Martha and Eleanor are working flat out in the hotel kitchen.

It is a large cavernous room, gleaming with steel fittings and white woodwork. Martha, putting the finishing touches to some plates of mixed salad and paté, says to Eleanor, 'I've nearly finished here. When Jeremy's sorted out the wine you can tell the Master of Ceremonies he can start getting the guests in.'

She glances towards her friend who is busy searching for something among the trays.

'That boy seems a bit fragile to me.'

'Perhaps he has something on his mind.'

'What are you looking for?'

'Martha, you did . . . remember to put in the salm . . . ?'

At this precise moment, Jeremy walks into the kitchent. His task so far has been to unload the wine from the cars and set out the bottles in the dining room.

'There's a case short, mum. I can't finish all the tables without it.'

Eleanor looks up: 'I know we brought the correct number. I checked the wine myself. Look under the bar. A case might have been put there by mistake.'

Meanwhile, Jill is chatting to Martin. On automatic pilot he continues to fulfil his duties as barman, while she babbles away. Martin's mind is a blank. The situation is so dire that he can't even begin to think what to do about it.

'Martin, are you listening to me?'

Her lover hands two glasses to the groom's older brother, a spotty faced youth, who is trying to figure out how he can slip out of the reception – say when the speeches start – without his parents noticing. There is a home game this afternoon and he might get to the ground by half-time if he's lucky.

'Of course, darling, but I am a bit busy at the moment.'

'And you haven't explained to me what you are doing serving behind the bar at the Crown.'

Martin decides that attack is the best form of defence and so counters, 'And you haven't explained to me what you are doing at this wedding.'

'Darling, I did say. Laura's wedding, I told you it was today.'

'Who's Laura?' enquires Martin, serving alco-pops to a pair of giggling bridesmaids (pink chiffon over white satin/rosebud head-dresses).

'Laura's my old school friend. I told you that she moved here from St Albans when I was in the sixth form. Hi Sharon. Hi Trish. See you in there.'

'Two sherries please and a tomato juice.' The bride's father, a saturnine, depressed looking man is demanding attention now. The unfortunate chap has every reason to be depressed. This wedding has set him back a 'cool' £17,000.

'Right sir.' Martin dispenses the drinks.

'Three pounds sixty-five please, sir. Thank you, sir.'

Jill sips her wine moodily as she watches Sharon and Trish sashay through the crowded bar. 'I wanted to be a bridesmaid, but seeing as Laura has whole cohorts of sisters and cousins . . . .' But she is interrupted by the fat man who has recognised Jill.

'Jill Peters! Laura said you were coming. She told me you'd moved here from St Albans as well. Lovely to see you again.' But the aristocratic blonde is not happy that her escort is talking to another attractive female. 'Michael!'

'Coming. See you inside, I daresay.' Fat man and blonde leave the bar and nearly bump into Jeremy.

'Dad! Have you got a case of white wine behind the bar? We're one short and . . . .'

Jill looks from Jeremy to Martin in astonishment. Martin avoids her eye and then spots his wife standing at the bar entrance.

'Last orders, Martin! We're getting everyone in to eat now.

Jeremy, come on! We're about to start serving.'

Jeremy's face has brightened at the sight of this pretty blonde. He produces his most winning smile, but Jill is not impressed.

'So this is young Jeremy,' She says coldly. Jeremy's smile falters.

Back in the kitchen, Eleanor continues to search. As her friend enters the room, she says anxiously, 'You're not getting them in?'

Martha, who has been over to the Master of Ceremonies to check arrangements, moves across the kitchen to collect a tray of glasses.

'The M.C. has lined up all the guests. They're going in.'

'But we will be short on the first course. I still can't find the salmon.'

'Well you brought them in your car.'

'I didn't.'

In the bar, Martin is lifting a case of wine over the counter to Jeremy. 'Is this what you are looking for?

'Thanks, dad. Are you going to introduce me to your friend?'

Jill, stony-eyed, says, 'Jill Peters, your father's secretary.' They shake hands.

One of the ushers, a white carnation in the buttonhole of his grey morning suit, rushes up to the bar. 'A vodka, two sherries, and a whisky please.'

Martin, quietly desperate, says, 'Bar's closing now, sir.'

'There's time for one more round. There's a good chap'

'Coming up, sir.' Martin pours the drinks.

Jeremy, who is still eyeing Jill with interest, says to his father, 'You should have finished serving drinks now. You'll cop it if mum . . . .'

Jill interrupts him. 'I can't tell you how pleased I am to meet you at last Jeremy. Are your brothers here, too?'

'Brothers?'

'That will be £15.40 sir.

'Lionel and . . . .'

The usher says, 'Got a tray?'

Martin places the drinks on a tray and then dispenses the change.

'Certainly sir. That will be £4.60 change, sir.'

At this point, an irritable Martha comes out to see what is going on. 'Jeremy! What's keeping you? Two tables are short of wine. Now listen. There's only soup and the salad and paté for starters, so don't be too generous with the helpings.'

Jeremy comes to attention. 'Sir.' He picks up the case of wine. 'Bye Jill. See you later perhaps.'

Now it's Martha's turn to comes to attention. 'Jill?'

Seeing that his father is incapable of speech, Jeremy makes the introduction. 'Jill Peters, dad's secretary.'

Martha is astonished and furious but she takes care not to show it. Instead she beams and say, 'What a pleasant surprise.' And to Jeremy: 'Well, why are you still hanging about? Go and give Eleanor a hand. I'll be right there.'

As he leaves, Jeremy asks plaintively, 'What happened to the salmon?' But receives no reply.

The bar has emptied now apart from Jill, slumped on her stool, and Martha, who is desperately trying to think of something to say. She glares at her husband but Martin is busy collecting glasses from the surrounding tables and pretends not to notice. He knows that Armageddon is nigh so when his wife coughs loudly, Martin returns reluctantly to the bar.

He doesn't say anything though, mainly because he can't think of anything to say.

As Jeremy enters the kitchen he almost collides with Eleanor who, carrying a tray of starters, is leaving. 'Mum said I was to give you a hand.'

'Serve the soup. I'll do the paté. You do look pale.'

'I feel pale what with one thing and another.'

Things are not going well at the bar. Jill is silent and Martin is busy polishing every glass in sight, including those that haven't been washed. In the end, Martha says, 'I'd better go. I'm sure you two have such a lot to talk about.'

Finally Jill speaks: 'Not really. In fact there's only one thing I've got to say and that is, it's off. Martin! I'm through! Finished. History. Do I make myself clear?'

'Crystal.'

'And that goes for the job too.' Martha can't believe her ears.

'Now don't talk like that. You two have something very special and . . . .'

'He lied to me Martha!'

'I know but I'm sure he had his reasons. That's why . . . .'

Eleanor appears at the entrance to the bar: 'Martha!' And disappears.

'Little Jeremy, indeed! How old is Lionel? Thirty-three? It's over. Do you hear?'

'Let's not be hasty. Say something, Martin!'

As she makes for the door, Martha calls urgently, 'Before you make any final decision just think about it, Jill.'

Jeremy is now standing in the bar doorway. 'Mum!'

'Look I have to go.'

Jill calls after Martha, 'I'm just sorry I tried to break up your marriage. When I think about how guilty he made me feel about those little boys.'

Martha calls as she makes her way out of the bar, 'But he

can explain all that, can't you, Martin?'

In the dining room everyone awaits the entrance of the bridal couple. At last the Master of Ceremonies calls; 'Put your hands together for the bride and groom.' And the pair enter to the sound of rhythmic clapping, stamping and cheering from the assembled guests.

Martha should be in the dining room herself now. She isn't. She can't tear herself away from ground zero and hovers in the doorway of the bar bleating ineffectually, 'I've really got to go.'

To her fury, Martin says, 'I'll come and give you a hand.'

'No, talk to her, Martin. I won't forgive you if you don't get this sorted out. Haven't you done enough for one day?'

'What else have I done?'

'You made me forget the salmon.'

As she leaves, Eleanor's voice shouts frantically from the dining room. 'Martha! Come on!'

Martin calls after his wife. 'Martha!'

Her irritated voice floats back: 'What now?'

'What do I say, Martha?'

'Think of something.'

In the dining room, Martha joins Jeremy and Eleanor who are busy serving the first course. Jeremy is hovering beside a blue-rinsed matron wearing dangling silver ear-rings and a purple frock, 'Paté or soup, madam?'

'There's salmon on the menu.'

Jeremy replies in a camp voice, 'Salmon's off, dear.'

Eleanor decides to let him off the hook: 'So is the engagement, buster.'

FIVE

June. Sunday morning

It is nine o'clock in the morning, one week after the wedding. The sun has been up for hours and is sending slanting beams of light through Martha's bedroom window. Oblivious to the golden light, Martha is lying in bed reading. She does not bother to look up from her book when Martin enters the bedroom door, carrying a large breakfast tray. Rolled up under one arm are the Sunday papers. On the tray are boiled eggs, toast, a cup and saucer, a coffee-pot, grapefruit in a cut glass dish and a rosebud in a tiny china vase. Looking expectantly at his wife, Martin places the tray on a table beside the bed. If he is hoping for thanks, Martin is about to be disappointed. Martha is not bought off so easily. Looking up from her book she says irritably.

'What's this?'

'Breakfast in bed.'

'I don't eat breakfast.'

'Grapefruit and . . . .'

'I hate grapefruit.'

'You like a lightly boiled egg.'

'For tea when I've got tonsillitis.'

'And there's toast and honey.'

'It's burnt.'

'You like it well done.'

'Not black.'

Martin knows when he's beaten. 'Here's the papers,' he says despondently and leaves the room.

Martha calls after him. 'You've started the crossword and two across is wrong. You know I don't like anyone . . . .' she tails off as he fails to reappear.

Telling himself that Martha will come round in the end, Martin resumes his ironing downstairs in the kitchen. One day at a time, that's the ticket. He selects a blouse from a basket of clothes and slowly and carefully begins to iron it. On the kitchen table is a radio/CD player with a pile of CDs beside it. Martin finishes ironing the blouse, hangs it over the back of a chair and, before selecting another garment, riffles through the CDs. He picks one and places it in the player. He has chosen a selection of hits from the eighties. Paul Garrack singing 'When you walk into a room' is the first number on the CD. Martin sings along loudly and off key as he continues to iron.

Martin – and Paul Garrack – are just getting into their stride when the door opens. Eleanor enters the kitchen. She is wearing a sleeveless, high-necked lemon cotton dress, white espadrilles and has gathered her hair into a pony tail. She looks not a day older than twenty-five.

'Martin, it's a bit loud.'

'Remember this one?'

'Not really.'

'It was our song.'

'I didn't know we had a song.'

'Mine and Martha's.'

'You and Martha had a song?'

Martin is ironing a pair of his wife's jeans now. Eleanor watches him critically for a minute or two and then says, 'Where is Martha, anyway?'

'Upstairs. I've just taken her breakfast in bed.' He finds a blue silk blouse in the basket and places it on the ironing board. Then he adjusts the heat on the iron and begins work on the blouse.

'She doesn't eat breakfast.'

'And now I am ironing her blouse.'

'She never wears that blouse. She hates it.'

'Then why is it in the basket?'

'She is sending all the clothes in that basket to Oxfam.'

'All of them?'

Martin stops ironing, dives into the basket and pulls out a shirt and an old pair of jeans.

'My old jeans! I don't believe it. My rugby shirt.'

Smiling to herself Eleanor mounts the stairs, passes the bathroom where the scent of salmon is now a distant memory and enters Martha and Martin's bedroom. Martha has abandoned her book and is attempting to do a crossword in the Sunday newspaper. She does not look up as her friend strolls over to the open bedroom window to admire the lilac tree outside. Eleanor drinks in the scent from the blossom for a moment or too, then goes over to the bedside table to examine the breakfast tray. She pours herself a cup of coffee, butters a slice of toast, and eats the grapefruit. Then she riffles through the sections of newspaper laid out on the bed. Finally she moves over to the swivel chair by the computer and settles down to read.

At last her friend looks up from her crossword and says peevishly, 'Don't mind me. Just help yourself. Actually, that was my breakfast.'

'You don't eat breakfast.'

'I know that. You know that. I'm pretty sure that Lucinda and Jeremy know that. So why I ask myself, hasn't Neanderthal man downstairs cottoned on yet? If he is trying to get back into my good books, this is not the way!'

Eleanor continues to leaf through the paper. Martha returns to the crossword.

'Reverse Communist goes east in party. Cancels smell.'

Eleanor thinks for a moment and then says, 'Deodorant. Want any more help?'

'I'd have got it eventually.' Martha writes in the answer to the clue.

Rising from her chair Eleanor begins to pack up the breakfast things.

'He's ironing the frilly blouse your Aunt Beatrice bought you last Christmas,' she says. 'And he's singing your song. I didn't know you and Martin had a song Martha.'

'Well there you are then. You don't know everything. We have a song. Why shouldn't me and Martin have a song?'

'When you walk into a room,' Eleanor sings mockingly.

'That's not our song. Our song was 'Babooshka', Kate Moss.'

Before Eleanor can reply, the sound of a Hoover comes floating up the stairs. This is too much for Martha. She thrusts the crossword aside and throws herself back among her pillows in frustration and rage.

'I can't take much more of this. He's driving me mad. He insisted on cooking the meal last night . . . .'

'What did he cook?'

'Beef Wellington.'

'I'm impressed. How was it?'

'OK but the pastry was a bit soggy. And he bought me flowers. Me! I told him . . . I said, "You should be sending Jill flowers. Not to your wife." He's not even trying to make it up with her. He's thrown in the towel.'

She settles herself more comfortably against her bank of pillow.

'Anyway, is this just a social call or are you here at. . .' she checks her watch, '. . . nine fifteen on a Sunday morning on the off chance of a bit of breakfast?'

'I've come to ask a favour as a matter of fact. You know we've got this mini lunch for tomorrow for the anaesthetists . . . .'

'Paediatricians.'

'Yes, whatever. Mushroom à la Greque, Mexican Chilli or Lasagne and Summer Pudding or Chocolate Gateaux.'

'No, I can't manage on my own.'

'Yes you can. Come on Martha. All the cooking is done. It's in the freezer.'

There is the sound of hammering from downstairs.

'God, what's he doing now?'

'He keeps mending things and putting up things and . . . . '

'What things . . . ?'

'Oh shelves and things.'

The hammering stops for a moment. Then it resumes. There is a crash, a shout of rage, followed by silence. Eleanor wanders round the bedroom picking up the clothes Martha has left on the floor and draped over the end of the bed. She folds and tidies.

'Well that's settled then. You'll manage without me tomorrow.'

'Will you stop doing that.'

'What?' Eleanor picks up a blue silk dress from the floor, moves over to the fitted wardrobe, selects a hanger and hangs it on the rail.

'Put it back.'

'Don't be silly. It was on the floor.'

'If you don't mind I will decide whether my dress stays on the floor or lives in the cupboard. The trouble with you is you're too damn bossy and interfering. Anyway why do you want tomorrow off? What treat has Hank . . . .'

'Luke'

'Whatever . . . got in store? Is he meeting you for lunch outside Parkhurst or is it the Scrubs after seeing . . .what does he call them?'

'His clients. Luke is a Probation Officer after all. He's taking me out into the country as a matter of fact.'

'Oh it's an Anti-Blood Sports demo again. That will be fun. Try not to get trampled on this time.'

'It's not a demo. He promised.'

'What is it then?'

'It's a surprise. I'm meeting him at some country house. We are having lunch there.'

'OK. I'll do the paediatricians on my own but you owe me and can pay me back next Saturday when I'll be needing a bit of help. I'm planning a little dinner party.'

'Where?'

'Here.'

'For you and Martin?'

'Don't be ridiculous. For Jill and Martin.'

Monday

At midday, while Martha is serving the paediatricians lunch in the consultants' mess at the local hospital, Eleanor is driving along a narrow, twisting country lane, high hedgerows on either side. She pulls the car onto the grass verge and studies the map. Satisfied that she is on the right track, she continues. Ten minutes later she arrives at a crossroads where there is a sign: FARTHINGALE HALL, COUNTRY FAIR. She turns left, following the arrow and finally arrives at massive wrought iron gates. Once through the gates the young woman finds herself on a curving drive, with open parkland on either side. At last she draws to a halt in front of an impressive white stone, Elizabethan house, fronted by sweeping lawns. To one side of the terrace are various other signs: DOG SHOW; SHOW RING; FLOWERS AND VEGETABLE CONTEST; ANIMAL CORNER and VISITORS CAR PARK.

Eleanor is just about to make for the car park when she hears the sound of an accordion. A dozen Morris Men appear from behind the house. They are dressed in white shirts and trousers with bells jingling at knee and wrist. Eleanor gets out of her car and as they pass, the last Morris Man tinkles up to her. He has a thin straggling beard, shoulder length brown hair, a long thin face, dominated by a long pointed nose and glasses. It is Luke.

'Hi El! You look gorgeous.'

Eleanor, dressed in a white sundress, splashed all over with large red poppies and white heeled sandals knows she looks gorgeous. She also looks annoyed.

'Why on earth are you dressed in that ridiculous get up? You never told me you went in for Morris dancing.'

'I don't. Mate of mine asked me to fill in for him. Seems he's broken his ankle. Chap thought of me because he knew I did a bit of country dancing.'

The rest of the troupe of Morris Men is disappearing round the other side of the house now. One calls out to Luke, 'Come on. We're on.'

'I thought it would be a surprise. I wanted to surprise you.'

'You've done that all right.'

Sarcasm is wasted on Luke. He beams and hands a battered package and two apples to Eleanor. 'And here's lunch. 'See you later.'

Eleanor drives round the back of the house and locates the car park where she parks her car. From the car park she can hear the sound of music. She follows a path, which leads along the side of a kitchen garden and comes out into a flagged courtyard. There is a crowd of people in the courtyard watching the performance of the Morris Dancers. Eleanor joins them. She finds herself next to a large noisy family – hearty track-suited dad and mum, a toddler with a runny nose, a whiney five-year old and a bored eight year old. Mum is unpacking a picnic hamper and handing out food. Eleanor opens up her package and glumly munches a sardine sandwich.

The older boy watches the dancers with contempt.

'They're useless,' he jeers. 'Especially that one.' He is pointing at Luke.

In the end she can't bear to watch any longer. Returning to the path through the kitchen gardens, she sees a sign that points the way to the show ring and follows it.

The sun, which has shone with such determination all morning, now decides it's time to go. Perhaps it was watching Luke dance. Anyway it disappears behind a large purple cloud. A chill wind whips across the field – laid out with a circle of rough hurdles – where Eleanor now finds herself. Urged on by her hearty looking parents, a fat little girl on a fat little pony is making her way purposefully towards one of them. Shouts of encouragement from a scattered crowd spur the child on.

'Come on Amanda.'

'Back straight, chin tucked in.'

'Knees. Knees.'

'I've been looking all over for you. Why did you wander off? You missed the Cumberland Heel Dance.' Eleanor is so cold and bored now that she is almost pleased to see her jingling friend again.

'After driving all this way?' but again her sarcasm is lost on Luke. 'Never mind I've seen the Show Jumping so all is not lost.'

'The thing is shall we have a look round the Home Farm now or would you rather see the organically grown fruit and vegetables before we eat?'

'Or there's the flower arranging and the pickles and jam competition. Spoilt for choice really,' says Eleanor. 'As a matter of fact I've already started on the sandwiches.'

'I knew you'd love it here. Better than some posh restaurant any day. And don't worry I've got plenty more sandwiches.'

Pulling a ruined heel out of a cow pat Eleanor says without hope, 'What's in the sandwiches?'

'Peanut butter.'

'Wicked.'

While Eleanor is 'enjoying' her outing to Farthingale Hall, Martha begins her campaign. Since the wedding, Martha has been brooding about the quarrel between Martin and Jill. She views the break-up as a challenge. One way or another she is determined to get her husband and his mistress back together again. And once Martha has embarked on any project, she is like a dog with a bone. There is no way that she will give it up. That's why, after the paediatricians' lunch, she goes to a florist shop and selects a dozen red roses. Then she visits a confectioner.

The opening shot of her campaign lands late afternoon. Jill is at home looking through the 'Situations Vacant' column of the local paper when she hears the doorbell. When she goes to answer it she finds a messenger holding a large bunch of flowers standing outside. Puzzled, she takes them from him and closes the door. Standing in her large oak-panelled hall, she takes out the card and reads it.

'I love you. I miss you. Martin.'

The second salvo arrives early next morning. Jill, who has only just got up, is sitting at the table in her kitchen, drinking her first coffee of the day, when the doorbell rings again. Dressed in a white lace trimmed negligee worn over a chiffon nightdress that barely covers her knees, she goes to the door and opens it. The postman, happily appreciating one of the perks of his job, hands her a large parcel. She takes it into the kitchen and removes the wrapping paper. Inside is a large box of Belgium chocolates. There is a card. It reads: 'Missing you. Loving you. Martin.'

Tuesday evening
Martin and Martha are in the kitchen. Martin is by the stove

stirring a cheese sauce. He has volunteered to cook the evening meal again. Martha is sitting at the kitchen table planning menus for the forthcoming week. The phone rings. Martin picks up the phone. It's their daughter, Lucinda.

'I'm thinking of coming home.'

'Well that's good news.' Martha raises her eyebrows enquiringly. Martin puts his hand over the mouthpiece again.

'She's leaving that trombone player.'

Martha puts down her pen. 'French Horn. He plays the French Horn.'

'Look, I'll put you on to mummy. She's so pleased. So am I. Shall I come to fetch you?'

Martha gets to her feet. 'You'll do no such thing.'

'Mummy? I'm holding the phone away so that you can hear it.'

The sound of a French Horn playing a slow melancholy melody floats into the room

'Can you hear?'

Martha says placidly, 'Yes dear. It must be Manfred practising. He plays very well. I have always liked the French Horn.'

'Well I don't. I hate it.'

'Only last week you said how much you loved it. You said it was so wonderful being with such a sensitive musician. You said . . . .'

'I never said sensitive. Musicians aren't sensitive. They are self-centred, and they drink too much . I can see now why his wife left him.'

'You must make allowances, artistic temperament and all that. These things take time.'

'Don't you want me to come home?'

There is a long pause. Of course Martha doesn't want her daughter to come home. 'Of course I do, dear. But I don't

55

want you to make a hasty decision that you might regret later. I mean you knew he was a professional player when you moved in with him.'

'It's not what I expected.'

'No dear. It never is.'

Wednesday

Martha and Jill are seated at a window table in an Italian restaurant in the High Street. It is a smart restaurant with shining black tiles; marble topped tables and photographs of Tuscany – yew trees, churches and hill towns – on the gleaming white walls. The two women have just finished their meal.

'That was lovely. It was sweet of you to invite me to lunch.'

In a dulcet voice that Eleanor would have difficulty recognising Martha says, 'It was sweet of you to come. I'm so glad we've had this talk. I felt you should know how badly Martin is taking the break up. He's moping about the house. He doesn't eat. He doesn't sleep. He's drinking. He's just not the same man since you split up. He's . . . he's . . . a shell. '

A dark eyed, Irish waitress clears the plates, listening to every word. She eyes the slim fair girl in the cream short skirt and the older woman in the lime green trouser suit with interest.

'Coffee?' She asks.

Martha looks enquiringly at Jill who nods, 'Two please. Black.'

'I want us all to be friends.'

'Good idea. Look. Come round for dinner on Saturday evening. And we'll all share a meal together.'

Jill looks doubtful. 'A meal with you and Martin? '

'The three of us will have a nice meal together, just to prove how adult we are. Is it a date?'

'I'd like that.'

SIX

Thursday afternoon

Martha and Martin's daughter, Lucinda, perches demurely on a piano stool before an upright piano in the sitting room of Manfred, her current partner's flat. She is dressed in a pink and white striped dress and has her fair hair tied back with a pink ribbon.

It is a brown room which reflects the taste of Manfred's first wife. There is a brown, three piece suite, brown curtains at the long sash windows, one brown wall and three beige-brown bookcases, brown-looking hunting prints, a large screen television and a piano. Manfred, no great shakes in the looks department, is seated opposite a music stand by the windows. He is thickset with thinning hair, heavy features and protuberant eyes. He took the part of Mr Frog in a school production of 'Wind in the Willows' when he was young and you can see why.

He is playing his French Horn now and suffering because Lucinda, a terrible musician, is attempting to accompany him on the piano. Finally she crashes up to the double bar and says, 'I think I'm beginning to get the hang of it now.'

Manfred lays down his horn, 'There's just one snag. You're murdering the second movement, while I'm attempting to play the third.'

Lucinda blinks and then rapidly turns the pages of her score. 'Third, third. Ah, I've got it now.'

Manfred picks up his horn again. 'Let's start at letter A, where I come in. Give me the bar before.'

Lucinda plays but stumbles and falters again and again. Suddenly Manfred's slim reserve of patience comes to an end.

'F sharp, F bloody sharp!'

'Don't shout, I'm doing my best. Anyway, I can't see an F sharp.'

'In the key signature. It's in the fucking key signature.'

Thursday evening

Martin and Martha finish their meal and settle down for the evening: Martin in front of the television and Martha with a book. Their sitting room is a comfortable, lived-in room with large squashy easy chairs, a Habitat settee, one wall of Ikea bookcases, a music centre and shelves of CD's, videos and DVD'S. Also on display are numerous family photographs of holidays in Cornwall, the Dordogne and Italy. In one photograph, Lucinda, a coy pony-tailed ten-year-old cuddles a Labrador. In another Jeremy, a skinny sixteen, is holding a large fish. Martin is half watching a travel programme on the television but he abandons it and decides to continue the pursuit of his wife's attention. He moves to sit by his wife on the settee, placing one tentative arm along the back. Martha looks at the arm for a moment and then shifts along the settee. 'How's the Ruth Rendell?'

'What?'

'How's the Ruth Rendell? The book you are reading. It's Ruth Rendell.'

'I know it's Ruth Rendell.'

'Is it good?'

'Very good.' She continues to read for a moment and then looks up to see Martin staring at her intently.

'What?

'I thought we could go to the pictures . . . say Friday or Saturday night.'

'You're asking me to go to the pictures with you!' She lays aside her book.

'What do you think of the "Cinema Today"?'

'Today?'

'The "Cinema Today". Like now.'

'I see. As opposed to say, yesterday.'

'Or say 10 years ago.'

'It's about that long since we went to the cinema together . . . longer. I remember we went to see "Kramer versus Kramer".'

'What are your views on Greenpeace and Global warming?'

'I thought we were discussing the "Cinema Today".'

'Don't you have an opinion about Greenpeace and Global warming?'

'Of course I have an opinion.'

'Then what is it?'

'Well . . . I think the Green movement is a very good thing, environmentally conscious and all that. I'm definitely on its, their side. Yes.'

'Would you vote Green at the next election if there were a local candidate?'

'I might.'

'What about the problem of the ozone layer, the greenhouse effect, pollution . . . .'

'Well I'm doing my best.'

'You mean the bottle bank.'

'I bought a new fridge. I use lead free petrol and I buy environmentally friendly washing powder.

'And that awful loo paper that scratches.'

'We all have to make sacrifices.'

'So the environment's in safe hands then. What about Buddhism?'

'We are having a wide-ranging discussion, aren't we?'

'What's your favourite colour?'

'I haven't got a favourite colour unless it's . . . anyway what's yours?'

'Blue.'

'Is it? I never knew that.'

'We've been married all these years and you still don't know my favourite colour. What football team do I support?'

'Liverpool.'

'Liverpool!'

'Well you did once.'

'Liverpool! Not me, never.'

'You're right. I was thinking of Kevin. I nearly married Kev.'

'You didn't marry him though, did you? You married me. It hasn't been so bad has it . . . by and large? We've had our ups and downs.'

'What ups?'

'Jeremy. Lucinda,' he says, a touch sanctimoniously.

'Not to mention Lionel and . . . .'

'That's all over.'

'Not necessarily.'

'You were there. She dumped me.'

'She'll get over it, in time. Anyway admit it, you want her back. You sent her flowers.'

'How do you know?'

'So did I.'

'You did what?'

'I told you. I sent her flowers. Don't worry, she thinks they came from you. I wrote a lovely message: - Loving you. Missing you. Martin.'

Martha looks at Martin but he just stares back at her. For once, she has no idea what he is thinking.

In the end she says, a bit lamely, 'On the card, that's what I wrote.'

At last Martin speaks: 'Why do you always have to interfere?'

'I thought if I left it to you, you and Jill would never get back together again. I sent her chocolates as well. They cost a fortune. Martin, why don't you go round to see her?'

'I've no intention of going round to see her. I only sent the flowers to say sorry for the silly lies. You've got to face up to it Martha, you're stuck with me.'

Martha smiles. 'Wanna bet?'

Eleanor is also at home on Thursday evening. She is lying on her immaculate white leather sofa in the kind of room you might find gracing the pages of a glossy magazine. There are tall white walls rising to a high ceiling, discreet lighting, a large black television, which she has just switched off, a low black coffee table on which stands a single ebony African sculpture, two straight backed ladder chairs and a black lacquer Chinese cabinet. Eleanor's mobile phone rings. She checks the dial.

'Luke?'

'Have I told you that you have a lovely voice.'

'No, I don't think you have.'

'It's low and sexy and just listening to it . . . can I come round?'

Eleanor smiles. 'No Luke. I've very tired and I have to be up early tomorrow. I was just about to go to bed.'

'The Morris Men have got a gig. We're booked to dance on Saturday night at the Pig and Whistle – that pub just off the by-pass. We're on at eight so if you and I get there at say seven, we can get in a few jars first.'

'Saturday? Sorry, darling. I can't come to see you dance on Saturday. I've promised to help Martha with a dinner party.'

'Where's the dinner party?'

'At her house.'

'That's a bit unusual isn't it?'

'I'll explain later.'

'The fellas will be disappointed. I told them how much you enjoyed their dancing on Monday.'

'I'm sorry Luke, but I can't let Martha down.' She pauses and then adds: 'Of course I know I'm missing a great treat.' Luke thinks about this for a moment. Perhaps even he can hear the irony in Eleanor's voice. Before he can reply she goes on, 'Luke, is this Morris dancing going to be a regular thing? I thought last time was a one off.'

'I dunno. Chap I replaced is still not fit. They say if I practise a bit more, I might get a regular place on the team. Can't you come on to the pub after you have helped Martha?'

'Sorry. Can't be done.'

'Well if the mountain can't come to Mohammed . . . .'

'What are you talking about?'

'See you Saturday. Bye.'

Saturday evening. 6.15 p.m.

Martha and Eleanor are in Martha's kitchen putting the finishing touches to the meal. Martha is standing by the stove, stirring a sauce, when she turns to El and asks her to keep an eye on the pan. 'I want to check the table again.'

Eleanor takes the wooden spoon from her and stirs. 'You've checked it three times already. It's only for Martin for Christ's sake.'

Ignoring her, Martha goes into the dining room. Eleanor calls after her.

'Where is he anyway?'

Adjacent to the kitchen, the dining room is a long narrow room with a high ceiling. It is uncarpeted. The floor, Martha's pride and joy, is pine. She and Martin stripped and polished it themselves in the early days of their marriage. The only furniture in the room is a long maple-wood table, laid at one end for two, six high-backed chairs and an old-fashioned dresser where an assortment of china and glassware is displayed. Martha has gone to a lot of trouble. There are snowy-white place settings and napkins, gleaming silver, crystal glasses, candles and a silver bowl of red roses. At a low table by the door she has placed a CD player and a tower of CD's. On entering the room Martha selects a CD and places it in the player. Music so romantic and seductive that it makes your teeth ache, fills the room. Then she checks a trolley, on which are laid coffee cups, a cheese board and a box of "After Eight's". Finally she moves over to the dresser. She selects a tall slender glass, fills it with water from the water jug and sets a long-stemmed red rose inside. She puts this glass by Jill's place.

Satisfied at last, Martha returns to the kitchen and says to Eleanor who is standing by a work top, chopping garlic, 'He's playing golf. He promised he'd be back early,' she says, opening the fridge and removing the oysters. She takes them over to Eleanor, who says anxiously, 'I cook the breadcrumbs in the garlic butter, top the oysters with the mixture and then pop the lot under the grill?'

Looking at her watch, Martha replies irritably:

'Yes, yes. I told you.'

'What if he decides to stay out and eat with his mates?'

'If you glance out of the kitchen door I think you will find that my husband's car has just pulled into the drive.'

Before Eleanor can reply Martha opens the door and goes outside to meet her husband.

'Martin! You're late. Where have you been?'

'I stopped to have a couple of drinks with the lads at the club. Is there a problem?'

'Okay, okay. Just go straight up and shower and change. Go on!'

Martin closes the boot and looks with astonishment at his wife.

'Shower? Change? Right now?'

Martha propels him towards the kitchen door. 'Don't argue. Just do as I say.'

The couple enter the kitchen. Martin says, 'Hi El. Something smells good.'

He takes the lid off a saucepan and sniffs appreciatively.

'There's "Crime of Passion" on at the Multi Complex. What say we go to pictures?'

'Pictures? Pictures? What do you mean "go to the pictures"?'

'Are you all right Martha? You look a bit flushed. Anything wrong?'

Martha runs her fingers through her wild mop of hair and says in a strained voice, 'Look, if you must know, I've arranged a little dinner party.'

'You never said. Who's coming? El?'

'No.'

'No. I'm the hired help,' grins Eleanor, pouring herself another glass.

'It's a dinner party just for two.'

Eleanor stands up and takes the oysters out from under the grill. Martin is touched. He goes up to his wife and puts both arms round her.

'You've cooked a special meal for you and me.' Eleanor places the oyster dish under his nose. He sniffs and pretends to swoon.

'Oysters! Mm.'

Martha says desperately, 'Please Martin! Go up and change.'

'Just give me five minutes.'

Martin bounds out and pounds up the stairs.

Before Martha can recover her composure there is the sound of the doorbell.

'That will be Jill,' says Eleanor with glee.

'Christ,' gasps Martha and runs to the bottom of the stairs.'

'Martin, do be as quick as you can.'

He calls down, 'Who's that at the door Martha? Shall I get it?'

'No, I'll get it. Just get showered and dressed as quickly as possible.' As Martha makes for the front door, Eleanor calls from the kitchen, 'I'm going. Bye Martin. Have a lovely evening.'

Martha smoothes down her hair, braces herself, and then opens the front door. Jill is standing outside dressed in a long flowery skirt and cream silk blouse. She is carrying a bunch of freesias.

'Hullo Jill, how lovely to see you. Are these for me? How sweet. Come in, come in.'

Martha leads the way into the sitting room and watches nervously as Jill wanders around. She examines the bookcase, admires the photographs before finally settling herself down on the settee.

'A drink. Let me get you a drink. What will you have?'

'White wine please.'

'Good idea. I'll have one too. Won't be a tick.'

Martha goes to the kitchen, pours out the wine and then returns to the sitting room, where she hands one glass to Jill.

'Well, this is nice.' At the same time as Jill says, 'What a pleasant room.'

Before the two women can continue their conversation they are interrupted by the voice of Martin, from above. 'Martha, Martha.'

With an apologetic smile Martha leaves the room and goes to stand at the bottom of the stairs. She looks up at her husband, who is standing on the landing in his boxer shorts, in despair and says in a bright artificial voice,

'Are you ready dear?'

'What shirt shall I wear?'

'The cream one.'

'It's not ironed. Shall I come down and . . .'?

'The pink one . . . the pink one.'

'Are you sure? I thought you didn't like the . . . .'

Martha turns her back and returns to the sitting room.

'Come with me to the kitchen and I'll show you where everything is.'

Jill, surprised but obedient, follows. Martha gestures to the grill, which is on a low setting. 'Grilled oysters for starters.'

Jill is astonished: 'Did Martin cook all this?'

Martha ignores the question. Instead she gestures inside the fridge.

'The white wine's chilling in here.'

And then opens the oven door. 'Here's the main course: a sort of sea-food casserole and the accompanying vegetables.'

Jill is bewildered. She says, 'It all looks very nice but . . . .'

Martha reopens the fridge. 'I forgot, there's a gateau or a fruit sorbet or a lemon soufflé for dessert and you'll find cheese and biscuits already out in the dining room, which is this way.'

A dazed Jill trots after Martha to the dining room, and watches as her hostess lights candles and puts another CD into the player. While Martha is fiddling with the player, Jill picks up her rose and holds it to her nose. At last she says, 'Um . . . lovely . . . but the table . . . it's laid for . . . . '

At this point Martin, hair still wet from his shower and wearing a pink shirt and beige slacks enters the room. He looks in amazement at his ex-secretary. She says shyly, 'Hullo Martin. You do look nice.' She goes up to him and kisses him on the cheek.

Martin is speechless. He looks from his wife, who is removing her apron, to Jill, and back again. Martha smiles and says, 'Well . . . then . . . I'll leave you to it. Bon Aperitif.' She exits the room quickly and as Jill and Martin stand gazing helplessly at each other, they hear the back kitchen door close.

Martin calls, 'Martha!' But it is too late. She has gone.

7 p.m.

Martha, a long, loose coat slung over her old jeans and tee shirt appears in the bar of the King's Head, one of three pubs in the High Street. Eleanor is sitting on a stool by the bar waiting for her.

'You didn't change then.'

'Couldn't, no time.'

'Well?'

Martha says to the barman, who is looking enquiringly at her. 'Large gin, small tonic please.' And to her friend, 'If he messes up this time, I'll never speak to him again.'

11 p.m.

In the Breman's sitting room, which is lit by a single lamp, smoochy music is playing. On a low table in front of the couch, where Martin and Jill are entwined, are two empty glasses and a half empty bottle of wine. With a sigh, they finally draw apart and Martin's fingers move determinedly to the buttons on Jill's blouse. He begins to unfasten them. Jill helps him.

'Oh Pooh,'

'Piglet. Darling piglet,' Martin undoes another button but Martha's husband is not feeling as enthusiastic about this whole enterprise as he should. He looks at the lovely girl in his arms and tries to work out what is wrong. It doesn't take him long. That he's here with his wife's blessing is what is wrong. It is Martha who has manoeuvred Martin onto this sofa. Martha has arranged for Jill to be lying in his arms. Knowing this somehow takes the shine off things.

'You're wonderful Pooh,' says Jill. Martin looks back on his relationship with Martha. Has she ever told him that he is wonderful? No she has not. To hell with Martha. Just stop thinking about the wretched woman, Martin tells himself. His hands move round to unfasten Jill's bra. She wriggles into a better position to assist him.

'I've missed you, Pooh.' With one hand grasping Jill's now

naked breast, Martin leans down to kiss her, a long lingering kiss. Finally they both come up for air.

'And I've missed my sexy piglet,' breathes Martin, fumbling with her skirt.

Suddenly everything is going along just fine.

'Anybody in? Mum? Dad? I'm home. Mum?' It is Lucinda's voice.

'Mum, I've left him, mum. I told him, I said, 'I'm not putting up with . . . . '

Lucinda, carrying a suitcase and dressed in a smart charcoal skirt and matching jacket, enters the room. 'It's a bit dark in here, you two.' She switches on the main overhead light and gazes in consternation at the settee. 'Dad!' She screams.

Martin leaps to his feet, his hand on his zip. Jill cowers back into the couch, trying to button her blouse.

'Now look here, Lucinda . . . .'

'I am looking, dad,' she says, pointing with a trembling finger. 'Dad, who is this . . . this . . . person?'

Martin walks over to his daughter, with as much dignity as he can muster in the circumstances. She backs away.

'You've got to understand Luce . . . your mum arranged every-thing. She knows all about Jill. Jill, this is Lucinda, my . . . .'

'I don't believe this is happening. Mum arranged this? You just have to be joking. Where is mum, anyway?' she says, looking round the room wildly. 'I refuse to believe this is happening. It's some ghastly nightmare. I'll wake up in a minute. Dad, how could you entertain this, this person in our home? It's sick! Wait until I tell mum!'

She does not have to wait long. Martha enters the room at this very moment and finds her carefully laid plans in little pieces all over her sitting room floor. Martha is so annoyed that for a moment she considers frog marching her daughter all the way back to Manfred's flat. She doesn't do this, of course. Instead she smiles sweetly and says, 'Ah, I see you've met Jill. Did you introduce Jill to Lucinda, Martin?'

Martin says with masterly understatement, 'I tried but Lucinda's a bit upset.'

Lucinda looks from one parent to the other in astonishment.

'Upset? Upset? Mum, I can't believe' – she's getting a bit repetitive but it's understandable in the circumstances – 'you know this . . . person?'

Jill has had enough. She pushes past the Bremans and makes for the door, sobbing wildly: 'Why does she keep calling me . . .' gulp . . . 'a person? I'm not a person.'

Martha is furious. All that planning, cooking, the flowers, the chocolates, all gone to waste. She makes one last frantic effort: 'Jill, wait! We can sort this out if we sit down and talk.' Then seeing Lucinda is about to start another tirade:

'Not another word, Lucinda. All this is none of your business. Anyway, what are you doing here at this time of night? I expect Manfred is wondering where you are.'

'I've left him, mummy. I . . . .'

Martha holds up her hand. 'Not now, Lucinda.' And then, glaring in exasperation at her husband who has collapsed onto the settee, 'And what are you laughing at?'

Martin looks from the furious face of his wife to the equally furious face of his daughter and tries very hard to contain his mirth. Only he can't. But he's the only person in the room that finds the situation amusing. Jill has stopped crying but gazes at her ex-lover, appalled. How can he laugh at her humiliation? What did she ever see in this awful man?

Martha shouts at her husband, who has found a handkerchief and is busy wiping his streaming eyes: 'For goodness sake, pull yourself together. Can't you see how upset the poor girl is? Say something to comfort her.'

Shoulders still shaking, Martin lurches to his feet, 'I'll see you out,' he manages at last, putting a placating hand on Jill's shoulder. She shrinks away.

'Don't touch me! I'm not . . . a person. Martin, tell her I'm not.'

'Don't go Jill. Martin, tell her she's not a person. Don't let her go like this.'

Lucinda who has listened to her parents' exchange in disbelief cries out; 'In a minute I'll wake up. Why doesn't someone wake me up?' Then, staring out through the French windows that overlook the rear garden of her home, she points a trembling finger. 'Oh God! I am going mad. Who on earth are those people? And what are they doing in our garden?'

They all turn to look out of the window. On the lawn outside, there is a troupe of Morris Men dancing. Luke is among them. He waves. Martin can't help himself. He waves back.

All bad things come to an end eventually. By just after midnight Martha has got rid of the Morris Men, Martin has driven his distraught ex-mistress back to her flat and Lucinda and her mother are standing outside their respective bedroom doors, about to retire for the night.

As she goes into her room Lucinda says icily to her mother, 'And who was that person?

Martha smiles grimly:

'If you hadn't frightened her away, she'd be your new stepmother.'

SEVEN

July. Monday evening

It is over three weeks now since the dinner party and once more the dust has settled. Martha and Eleanor are working in Martha's kitchen as usual and have just finished packing the food and equipment for their next assignment into boxes and onto trays.

'You load the dishwasher and I'll swab down the decks.'

'OK and while we're working we decide the menu for the Rugby Club Dinner on Friday. We should keep it simple, because they are holding it at their clubhouse and from what I remember, the kitchen there is a bit primitive. How about Vegetable Lasagne as the main course?'

Martha leans on her mop and stares at her friend in amazement.'

'You are joking of course.' Eleanor stares back.

'Eleanor, we've already decided the menu.'

'You decided you mean and what you decided is boring: Steak Tartare, peppered steak or possibly straight steak and chips. Blood oozing from the meat, of course.'

'What's wrong with that?'

'Why not be really original? How about lentil salad with walnuts and goats cheese for starters and roasted vegetable and brown rice gratin or we could do nut cutlets.'

'It would get round you know if we cooked nut cutlets for the Rugby Club Rage. I doubt if we'd work again.'

Eleanor tries to interrupt before her friend gets a full head of steam: 'Listen, Martha..'

But it's too late

'Why is it being held at the clubhouse? I'll tell you why. Their do's are notorious and you know it. When that lot get going they make the average Roman orgy look like a WI tea party. No hotel in town will have them after what happened at the Grand.'

'That was three years ago now. Ancient history. Everybody's forgotten.'

'The head waiter hasn't forgotten. You don't forget being stripped naked and dyed purple in a hurry. His large extended family hasn't forgotten either. I was only talking to his Auntie Rita the . . . .'

'These affairs get exaggerated. Anyway Luke says it's a reformed club these days, very PC. Trev, a friend of his, plays scrum half.'

'One swallow doesn't make a summer. A leopard doesn't change its spots.'

'A rolling stone gathers no moss.'

'They'd only have to read the words *vegetarian lasagne*, and they'd start tearing the place apart. Most of them think spaghetti is sissy, for God's sake. We're talking about the rugby club here, not Great-Bunting-Under-the-Marsh flower arranging soirée, or Missingdon Morris Men's macramé class.'

'That's below the belt.'

'Let's not make things complicated, El. If we have the chance of doing a nice straight forward meat and chips menu, let's take it'.

Eleanor has finished stacking the dishwasher now. She fills the kettle and takes two mugs from their hooks.

Martha begins to wipe down the work surfaces. As she works she goes into the attack: 'Luke's behind this isn't he? Just because he's a vegetarian you decide you have to be one too. It's pathetic.'

'There are ethical reasons,' says Eleanor grinding coffee beans.

'It's me you're talking to, El. Martha who has known you

since you were in the first year and she, remember, was in the fourth. Martha, who has watched your numerous boy friends come and go and all I'm saying is: you don't have to metamorphosis yourself into a carbon copy of every fella you go out with.'

'Sometimes I agree with Luke's opinions and sometimes I don't.'

'The trouble is that he has opinions on just about everything: animal rights; gay rights; plant a tree; save a penguin.'

'I happen to agree with him about animal rights and the environmental issues.'

'You're a chameleon, that's what you are.'

'Rubbish.'

'Did you or did you not go on that demonstration against hunting with hounds the week after you met him and the week after that you were demonstrating against the bypass round the bypass. Nothing like that was on the agenda BL.'

'What do you mean: B.L?'

'Before Luke. Did you prance round at ceilidhs BL? You used to eat beef so rare it was barely off the hoof BL. Now you're tucking into lentil bake on a regular basis while dancing the Cumberland Clog Dance.'

'Now look Martha . . . .'

'You're always same. Remember that company director you hung out with for a year or so – at least he was rich. What was his name? Giles or was it Rupert? He played golf.'

'You mean Gordon.'

'Gordon, right. When you were at school you were always skiving off games. Christ, you got tired playing snakes and ladders. Then along comes Gordon and you're lecturing me and Martin on birdies and practising putting on our sitting room carpet. Then you met Carl at your Yoga class.'

'Winston.'

'Winston, the Buddhist.'

'He was a Shinto Buddhist. There is a difference you know.'

'Suddenly you're lolling around in the lotus position and chanting mantras.'

'You can't loll in the lotus position, actually.'

'You even considered shaving your head.'

'I never did.'

'Well I remember saying to Martin, "She'll be shaving her head next". Don't come telling me that this latest vegetarian fad hasn't something to do with lover boy, Luke.'

The kitchen door opens and Luke, wearing knee length shorts, a brown smock-like over-shirt, open toe sandals and a large, toothy grin, strides into the room right on cue. He is carrying a largish leather holder – for his recorders – and a music case.

'Hi guys.' He kisses each woman in turn and then reaches down a mug and holds it out to Eleanor. Glaring at him, she pours out coffee from a cafeteria.

'I've just mopped this floor,' says Martha.

Luke ambles round the kitchen for a moment or two. He is the kind of man that can never keep still for two minutes together

'What are you doing here?'

Luke looks hurt. 'What do you mean, what am I doing here? It was what we arranged. You told me to come to Martha's straight after recorder rehearsal. You said that we should go out for a meal. Don't you remember?'

'I remember perfectly, but it never occurred to me that you would. You never remember. I've lost count of the times I've hung round waiting for you to show up.'

Luke walks over to her, places his hands round her face, and then bends over and kisses her. 'You must love me to put up with it.'

Eleanor smiles and stands up. She puts both arms round

her boyfriend and kisses him back. Martha looks on disgustedly.

'Not in my kitchen. Please.'

Eleanor goes over to the dishwasher, opens it and puts powder into the dispenser. Meanwhile, Luke has taken a descant recorder out of his case. He begins to play a dancing tune that sets Martha's feet tapping. Luke plays very well.

As he finishes with a flourish, Martha, who has listened appreciatively to his performance, says, 'I used to play the recorder . . . at school. Remember, El? I even continued when I went to the comprehensive. I was pretty good. I played in the school recorder consort at concerts and things. I was very pally with the music mistress for a time.'

'Until she asked you to turn over the music for her, when she was playing the organ in the school carol concert and you pulled out the trumpet stop while she was playing the *O silently* verse of *O little town of Bethlehem.*'

Luke is just beginning to play *O little town of Bethlehem* when the kitchen door opens and Jill enters. She is wearing a short white skirt and green crop top and looks as fresh as a meadow in springtime. Luke eyes her appreciatively as she stands hesitatingly for a moment in the doorway. Martha takes her hand and draws her into the room.

'Jill, what a lovely surprise. Let me introduce you to my partner, Eleanor, and her boyfriend, Luke.' Luke begins to play *Greensleeves* on his recorder.'

Luke stops playing, and waves the instrument. 'Hi Jill.'

'I play the recorder. I used to play with a group in St Albans,' says the young woman, shyly.

'Can you play sop?'

'I play all the recorders. I have a bass somewhere.'

'How about coming along to play next Monday?'

'You play the recorder?' Martha is surprised.

'I've played since I was seven.'

'You don't look like a recorder player.'

Martha sits down at the table and gestures to Jill to sit opposite. 'I'm so glad you dropped by. Have you come to see Martin, only I'm afraid. . . .'

'No, Martha. It was you I came to see.'

Eleanor takes the hint. 'Come on, Casanova. Time we were off. Nice to meet you, Jill.'

As he is dragged out of the kitchen Luke calls to Jill. 'Monday nights. 6.30 till 8. We rehearse at the Community hall in Raffles Street. We're playing the Capriol Suite among other things at the moment. Come next week. I'll look out for you.'

'I will,' says Jill.

As the door closes behind Luke and Eleanor, the young woman turns to Martha and says her piece:

'I've been meaning to come to see you for days, but it's taken all this time to get up the courage. I've wanted to apologise for dashing off that Saturday night and also I wanted to say thank you for the lovely meal you went to so much trouble to prepare. It was very rude of me not to come before.'

The young woman makes this speech so sweetly and sincerely, that for a moment Martha is touched. Suddenly she begins to see why Martin was drawn to the girl.

'I am so sorry that Lucinda upset you,' she says gently.

'Is she here now?' Jill looks round nervously.

'She and Martin have gone to collect the last of her things from her ex-boyfriend's flat. She's living here for the moment but I expect it won't be for long. I'm hoping that she and Manfred will eventually get back together.'

'Right.' Jill gets to her feet. 'I mustn't stop. I expect you are very busy.'

But Martha is unable to let her go so easily: 'Such a pity about you and Martin.'

Jill is standing by the door now, her hand on the door handle. 'It's all too complicated. Too many people are involved. You, of course, and now I've upset Lucinda.'

'She has a very sharp tongue has Lucinda. And she's bossy. I can't think where she gets it from. Look my dear, I wish you and Martin . . . .'

'No. This time it's really over. I weakened on that Saturday night. He, he was so sweet. You both were, but it's not to be. I have come to terms with that now.'

'Well there's always the recorder group to help you take your mind off things.' Then, more to herself than to Jill, 'Pity Martin doesn't play.'

Jill puts on a brave smile. 'Yes, I shall have to start practising again.'

Suddenly Martha has an idea: 'Jill, are you doing anything on Friday night?'

'If you have another little dinner party in mind, I think I will pass.'

'Oh no, nothing like that. It's just that Eleanor and I are catering for the rugby club dinner on Friday and we really could do with a hand. There's no dishwasher in the club room kitchen, so it will be mainly washing up I'm afraid. I suppose it's a bit of a cheek to ask but . . . .'

'I'd be glad to,' says Jill quickly.

'Good. I'd really appreciate it.'

As the door closes behind the young woman, Martha mutters to herself:

'Must make sure that Martin gets an invitation to the rugby club dinner.'

Martha is plotting again.

EIGHT

Tuesday. Late afternoon

Martha and Eleanor are working. They have just arrived at the club house and are about to discuss the menu of the forthcoming dinner with the rugby captain. Martha, Eleanor and Nigel, the captain, are sitting on grey plastic chairs around a small Formica topped table. The club house, a large wooden hut, is not the ideal venue for a dinner. Martha tries hard not to look at the walls. The sight of them makes her feel physically sick. In a misguided attempt to liven the dismal place up, some fool has painted them an eye-aching florescent green. She tries to concentrate on the club notice board opposite. Pinned to it are team and fixture lists and a large calendar showing a naked blonde with astonishingly large breasts reclining on a rug. In the corner opposite the outside door is a bar and next to the bar is another door, which leads to a small kitchen. The three round the table are silent because the captain is reading the menu that Martha has just handed to him.

The captain, a large man in his late thirties, reads slowly and carefully. Martha can see that his lips are moving as he scans the page. He seems totally absorbed so she can examine this stereotype rugby player at her leisure. All he is wearing is a white string vest and a grubby pair of mud colour shorts so that she can feast her eyes on his thick knotted arms and the black curly hairs on his muscular chest.

Finally he looks up and says slowly, 'Yes. This seems to be fine, by and large; all things considered, though, if you don't mind me saying so, a bit . . . a teensy bit . . . .'

The captain has a broad, brown face with deep set brown eyes and a long, thin, slightly crooked nose. The man's attractive if you go for the rough diamond type. Martha takes the menu from him and asks sharply, 'A teensy bit what?'

He leans back in his chair, folds his arms and puts his feet on the table, 'Well, predictable, if you know what I mean. Meat, chips . . . .'

'Prawn Cocktail as a starter . . . .'

'Exactly.'

'I thought . . . .' The captain leans back even further. The chair is balancing on two legs now. Eleanor watches hopefully.

'I know what you thought. Rugby players, all that macho types, nothing too subtle required, red meat men. Am I right or am I right?'

'You're right. I did try to tell her,' says Eleanor.

'Some of us are a little more discriminating you know. I, for example, pride myself on being something of a gourmet. That's why I came to you. I was given to understand that 'Martha's Kitchen' specialised in food for the connoisseur. Isn't that what it says in your brochure?'

He brings the chair back onto four legs and leans across the table and stares challengingly at Martha. 'Well, yes . . . but . . . .'

'I cook you know. My Prawn Provencal . . . well! Scrum half says he'd kill for it.'

'Do you cook vegetarian food?' Asks Eleanor.

'I make a wonderful vegetarian goulash.'

Martha looks at him in disbelief. 'Goulash?'

'But yes. I substitute smoked tofu for the meat and add a dash of cayenne to the paprika and just one chopped green chilli - de seeded of course and a clove of garlic. Chopped, not crushed.'

Martha is on the ropes. She says weakly, 'I see. Then are we to re-do the menu?'

The captain smiles. The smile opens up his entire face and reveals charming laughter lines at the corners of his eyes. Has he been teasing them all along? Eleanor is not sure, but she finds herself grinning back. The man's not bad looking at all.

He says, 'Perish the thought. Just make sure there are alternatives for the non-carnivores. Now let me tell you about my lentil bake. Got a pen?'

Tuesday evening

It is, unusually a warm Summer's evening and both Martin and Martha are in their garden. It is a lovely garden with a deep curving herbaceous border of lupins, wallflowers, roses, fuchsia, tall lilies and clumps of London's Pride and aubrietia. There are two apple trees, a laburnum, a grape that Martha is training up the side of the potting shed and a clematis, which has draped itself over the kitchen window. And a lawn and patio.

Martha is kneeling by one of the flower beds weeding, while Martin is sitting in a deckchair on the patio reading the Sunday paper. Yes, I know it's Tuesday, but Martin is a slow reader. He finishes the article finally and for a few minutes watches his wife weed.

Martin is under the delusion that his life is returning to normal. In one way he is sorry that the dinner party that his wife arranged for him with Jill ended in disaster, but in another he is relieved. The affair with his secretary was getting too complicated by far. Perhaps it's just as well that Lucinda came in when she did. Now Martha seems to have accepted the fact that his little liaison is finally over. Lucinda is home again. It's summer and he has just eaten an excellent meal. All is well with the world. He looks at his wife with affection.

'In some ways you're right. I see that now.'

'What do you mean "I'm right"?'

'About not really knowing you.'

Martha looks up from her replanting in surprise as her

husband reads out from the article he has been studying. 'Marriage should be a continuous voyage of discovery. Think of your partner as a whole continent to be explored. Whole areas can be discovered and rediscovered.'

'I know you, all right,' says his wife, grimly: 'Every hillock, headland, heath.' And then, warming to her theme: 'Every promontory, plateau, peninsular. Every . . . .'

'All right. All right. What you have failed to grasp is that you are talking about the surface.'

'And that's not a pleasant sight. Martin, I've asked you before not to wear those awful trousers. Apart from anything else they're too tight.'

As his wife continues with her weeding, Martin says solemnly, 'Martha. I think the time has come for us to reassess our relationship.'

Martha is not listening, 'Mm.'

He is reading again from the newspaper article: *Explore new interests together.'*

She is now. She stands, brushes soil off her trousers, walks over to her husband and sits down in an adjoining deck chair.

'That's right, Martin. I agree.'

Martin is delighted. 'You do? You think we should reassess our relationship?'

'That, yes, but what I'm really keen on is the idea or our exploring a new interest together.'

Martin is touched. 'Are you really, Martha? Let's see.' He mulls it over: something we could do together. Oh I know, you could take up golf.'

'No Martin. I'd be just sharing one of your interests.'

Martin knits his brow. 'We could learn a foreign language together, say Russian or Japanese.'

Martha looks very doubtful. 'Neither of us is very good at languages. I've got a better idea. We'll learn the recorder.'

Now it's Martin's turn to look doubtful. 'The recorder?'

'Yes. Why not? Come on. Let's give it a go. I can already play a bit and I've got a couple of descants somewhere. We'll start right now.'

Before he realises it, Martin is sitting in front of a music stand with a recorder in his mouth.

Wednesday morning

Lucinda has carried a basket full of clothes into the sitting room and set up the ironing board by the window. She takes out a sheet, drapes it over the ironing board and begins to iron. Martha enters the room and looks with disapproval at her daughter ironing. She bites her lip though, settles down on the sofa and picks up the morning paper. Glancing up some minutes later, she sees that Lucinda is now removing a towel from the basket of ironing. Under her mother's studied gaze the young woman arranges it carefully on the board and begins to iron.

Martha can contain herself no longer: 'That's a towel, Lucinda. I don't iron towels.'

Lucinda finishes ironing the towel, folds it carefully and then places on top of the already folded sheet. 'I iron towels,' she says, as she puts another one across the ironing board.

'And before that you ironed a sheet, a drip-dry sheet. No one irons sheets.'

'I iron sheets,' says Lucinda. She smoothes down the snowy white apron she has placed around her waist. Her smooth fair hair tied back into a pony-tail, Lucinda contrives to look both self righteous and efficient at the same time.

Ignoring her mother – she is really throwing the gauntlet down now – Lucinda selects a pair of knickers from the basket and begins to iron them. And of course is delighted when Martha rises immediately to the bait.

'I've never ironed a pair of knickers in my life,' she says, retreating to the sofa.

'You didn't iron my school blouses either,' says Lucinda.

'I did, sometimes.'

'Never; and I not only went to school in creased blouses but nine times out of ten you forgot to wash my PE kit as well.'

'But, Lucinda, even the deep psychological scar that I've clearly inflicted by my neglect can't have driven you to ironing your knickers!'

Lucinda takes another sheet from the pile and lays it out on the board.

'Strange as it may seem, I like sleeping between ironed sheets. I like drying my face on an ironed towel and wearing well pressed knickers.'

Martha sighs and then says patiently, 'I can see that it is necessary to react in some way against your upbringing. Everyone does, but you don't have to go to extremes. I'm an atheist for example but that doesn't mean you have to become a born again Christian.'

'And that's another thing. You didn't even have either me or Jeremy christened. I don't know anybody else who isn't christened.'

'Well, it's all coming out of the woodwork, now isn't it? Is that a problem? Not being christened?'

Martha closes her eyes as Lucinda takes a flannel out of the basket, saying: 'It might be. If I wanted to get married in church, it might be a problem.'

Martha brightens up. 'Are you and Manfred thinking of getting married? I'll arrange your christening straight away. You are quite right, I should have had it done along with the vaccinations and fluoride treatment.'

But Martha's hopes are dashed to the ground as Lucinda says irritably, 'I'm not thinking of getting married. I was just making the point.'

She folds the flannel carefully and begins to iron a tea-cloth. 'I'm not likely to get married. It's enough to put anyone off marriage watching the way you and dad carry on.'

Martha can't believe her ears: 'It's your father that's been carrying on, not me.'

'Yes, I know, and he should be ashamed. But you encouraged him. It's not natural. Most women would be very upset.'

'Well I'm not and I don't intend to pretend just to make you feel more secure.'

Lucinda is not only a conventional young woman she is also a stubborn one.

'Well I think you should be. Don't you care about daddy any more?'

'Of course I care about him. I'm devoted to him . . . in my way. I just don't want to go on living with him. Now that he has found someone who does, I am happy for him.'

Lucinda sighs. 'How could you think about arranging a dinner party for them both, here in this house?'

'It seemed a good idea at the time and it would have worked too, if you hadn't come barging in. Still all is not lost, not by a long chalk.'

Lucinda puts down the iron and glares at her mother: 'Now what are you plotting?'

Martha smirks but makes no reply.

After a pause Lucinda says, 'Will you answer this question then? Why, after 25 years, are you teaching my father the recorder?'

Martha says innocently, 'He wants us to explore some new interest together.'

When her daughter fails to reply, she retires behind the paper, saying, 'Manfred rang last night incidentally, after you had flounced off to bed.'

Lucinda goes pale. 'What did he say?'

Martha looks for a moment at her daughter's unhappy face and then she leaves the room, only to return a few minutes later with a suitcase. Lucinda, a bit at a loss, stands to one side watching her mother sort through the ironed clothes.

'He said that he misses you and he wants you to come back.'

'I miss him.'

'I know you do. That's why you've done all this ironing.'

'He was nasty about my piano playing.'

'That's understandable, my dear. I often felt like being nasty about your piano playing.'

'You should have made me practise.'

The door bell rings as Martha is saying, 'Both of my children have been a great disappointment to me – musically speaking.'

'What shall I do, mum? I feel a bit silly going back with my tail between my legs.'

'The first thing to do is to let him in. I rang him this morning and told him to come round to pick you up.'

Thursday evening

On Thursday evening, Martin is having his third lesson on the recorder. At the two earlier sessions, Martha taught him where to place his fingers to achieve the notes: G, A, B, C, D. Note-reading from the stave is a problem so his wife has printed the letters above the notes for the time being. All this makes it sound as if Martin is making progress. This is not the case. At present he is attempting to play *Go Tell Aunt Nancy*. He stops every second to peer accusingly at the music. Martha is standing next to her husband, trying not to scream. Finally she puts up her hand to stop him playing and says through gritted teeth: 'I am going to play the piece through correctly, Martin. Listen, watch and then do it again exactly the same.'

Martha raises her own recorder to her lips, plays the piece

through perfectly and when she has finished says, 'Your turn. Play it through like that.'

Martin is hurt. 'I did.'

'No you didn't, Martin.' She sings to him:'B 2, B, A, G 2, 3, 4, A 2, A , C, B, A, G.' And then bellows: 'You've just got to count!'

'How can I count with a recorder in my mouth?'

'In your head, Martin, count in your head. Try again.'

Martin sighs and has another go but after a couple of bars he stops playing and says plaintively, 'Can I play *London's burning?* I can play . . . .'

'Martin!'

NINE

Friday evening. 10.30 p.m.

It is the evening of the rugby club dinner and the meal is over. In the small kitchen behind the club-room Martha, dressed in jeans and a blue tee shirt, is washing up. At the sink beside her stands Jill with a tea-towel in her hand. Like Martha, Jill is wearing jeans and a tee shirt but whereas Martha's clothes are creased and grease-stained, Jill's green and white striped top is immaculate as are her designer jeans.

The room is dank and poorly lit from one naked bulb in the centre of the low ceiling. There is an old-fashioned butler's sink and draining board under the one small window and a long trestle table, piled with boxes, trays, washed crockery and uneaten food in the centre of the room.

As she finishes washing up, Martha begins to fill the trays and boxes with equipment, left over food, cutlery, crockery and glasses. She works quickly and efficiently, ignoring the noise from the next room: outbursts of song, cat-calls, raucous laughter, an occasional crash. She pauses though at the sound of running feet. Eleanor, a flushed, angry Eleanor, sweeps into the room so quickly that she nearly collides with the table. She is wearing black velvet trousers, a sleeveless black top and is carrying two coffee jugs. She slams the coffee jugs down onto the draining board.

'That's it! I'm not going in there again. I've had enough of being felt up and pawed.'

Martha placidly continues to pack glasses into one of the boxes. Nervously, Jill picks up the coffee jugs and rinses them out at the sink. Eleanor pours herself a glass of water, downs it in one and then sinks onto the only chair in the room. The noise from the adjacent room grows louder: The sound of stamping feet and thumping hands on tables accompanies the chanting 'DOGGA, DOGGA, DOGGA, OGGA, OGGA, DOGGA! GRUNGE.' The sound dies away and then crescendos again. Eleanor rises from her chair, goes over to the sink and pours herself more water. Then she puts her face under the tap and allows the cold liquid to trickle down her neck.

Unruffled Martha begins to tick off the contents of the boxes against a list.

'What you have to appreciate is that men are tribal animals, what with their slogans and their team games. I'm surprised an anthropologist hasn't written a paper on the subject.'

Eleanor rinses her hands and arms with water. 'You can afford to philosophise tucked away safely here in the kitchen. You wouldn't find it so easy if you were being chased by Picts and Jutes.'

Giggling nervously, Jill dries the last plate and then begins to help Martha fill the remaining empty boxes with crockery.

Leaving the final packing to Jill, Martha begins to stack the boxes next to the rear door of the kitchen, ready for loading into the car parked outside. 'I hope you didn't get nasty, Eleanor. I remember what you were like on the hockey field.'

'I only kicked one and kneed another.'

At this point the captain, looking very attractive in his immaculate dinner jacket and bow tie, enters the room. He glances anxiously towards Eleanor. 'Are you all right? The lads get a bit spirited when they've had a few.'

The tribal chants have changed into ragged singing now. There are two rival factions. One lot is bellowing, *My way*, and the other, *You'll never walk alone*.

Eleanor refuses to reply so Martha says politely, 'How's the chap she kneed?'

'I expect he'll be all right in the morning.' Then, to Eleanor, who is still leaning over the sink. 'If you come back in, they'll apologise. Even the chap you kicked is sorry for putting his hand on your . . . .'

Eleanor turns her back on the captain, picks up one of the boxes by the door and marches outside with it. Jill picks up another box and follows her. As the two young women disappear, Martha says, 'Don't worry, she'll get over it.'

The captain, his eyes on the door through which Eleanor has vanished, mutters absently, 'Lovely meal. The mushrooms in garlic were much appreciated by the lads.'

'I did wonder. Only they did throw them about rather a lot.'

Eleanor re-enters the room, picks up another box and as she leaves says laconically, 'The stripper's arrived,' and disappears again, followed by Jill who picks up a tray and leaves with her.

Martha raises her eyebrows at the captain as the shouts and whistles from the club room crescendo once again: more 'Ogga Ogga' and 'Get your tits out for the lads.'

He makes a hesitant step towards the door. Naturally he can't wait to get back to the action and equally naturally Martha is determined to thwart him. She says, 'What did you think of the hazelnut meringue? I would really value your opinion.'

Amused, she watches as the captain edges his way towards the partly opened door leading into the club room. Every now and then he manages to catch a tantalising glimpse of naked thigh as the stripper struts her stuff.

'Perhaps you had the lemon soufflé.'

There is a roar from next door. The stripper is discarding her bra now. The captain knows she has reached this stage of her act because he sees the garment as it flies past the door. Eleanor comes back into the room as he finally reaches his goal. She makes her way to the boxes of crockery and is about to lift one, when Martha administers the coup de grace.

'Be an angel and help us get this stuff into the car. Jill's out there. She'll tell you were everything goes.'

With a last despairing look towards the club room, the captain does as he is told. With ease he lifts two boxes and takes them out to the car.

Martha grins meaningfully at Eleanor who is unimpressed. She says coolly to her friend,

'You persuaded Jill to slave here tonight because Martin was coming, didn't you? Last time I was in there, he was leading the *My Way* rabble and conducting them with one of our best serving spoons.'

Martha looks shifty. 'Perhaps it might be just as well if the reunion was postponed to another occasion.'

As Jill returns to the room with the captain, Eleanor is saying sarcastically, 'An occasion when he's not drunk as a newt you mean.'

Before Martha can think of a suitably crushing reply, her husband and his ex-mistress do have the chance to meet. Martin doesn't spot Jill at first. This is because he enters the kitchen on all fours. Riding on his back is the stripper, stripped to the buff.

Half an hour later, Martha and Eleanor are on their way home. They have dropped a pale and subdued Jill outside her flat and are now making their way to Eleanor's flat. Martha is driving, and as she stops at a set of traffic lights, she begins to hum. Eleanor, who has been savouring that wonderful moment when Martin trotted into the kitchen with the stripper on his back, looks at her friend with irritation. 'Do you have to do that?'

Martha stops humming, 'Not if it annoys you, my dear.' She smiles so sweetly that Eleanor is immediately suspicious. She is also disappointed. Martha should be crushed.

'What are you up to?'

'Whatever can you mean?'

'You have no reason to smile. You should be fed up. Your little dinner party failed.

Lucinda is back home. And Jill will never want to see your husband again after what she saw tonight. Your pathetic little plan didn't work Martha.'

Martha negotiates a round-a-bout and says smugly, 'Not necessarily. Nothing's certain in this life. That's one lesson I have learnt. Anyway, Jill's broad-minded, I'm sure. She'll get over it. I'll just have to go to plan B is all. And as for Lucinda, she and Manfred left this morning. Didn't I say?'

'How did you manage that?'

'What a suspicious nature you have. I didn't do a thing. It was just a lover's tiff. She missed him. He missed her. Simple as that.'

'And you had nothing to do with the reconciliation?' Suddenly two drunks lurch off the pavement in front of the car. Martha has to swerve quickly to avoid them.

'It's their lives. I don't believe in interfering. You know that.'

Martha drives in silence for a moment or two and then Eleanor says sarcastically.

'And how are Martin's recorder lessons going?'

'Very well . . . all things considered.'

'It won't work you know.'

'What?'

'Plan B.'

'What plan B? I've got no plan B. You must have misheard me.'

'You've always got a plan B, only this one is even more bizarre than usual.'

'I have no idea what you are talking about.'

'Come on. This is Eleanor sitting here.'

'So. Tell me what Machiavellian plot I am hatching now?'

'Martin learns the recorder. He joins the Recorder Orchestra. Then, surprise, surprise, he encounters Jill. Their eyes meet across the music stands. 'Jill,' he cries. 'Martin,' she trills. That's about as likely to happen as President Bush quoting Proust.'

TEN

August. A few weeks later.
Sunday afternoon

It is a hot day in early August. The sun is blazing down on an astonished Britain from a Mediterranean blue sky. House martins and swallows are practising their fancy swoops and dives. Bees amble from blossom to blossom and in the distance can be heard the low drone of a lawn mower. Martha and Eleanor, sun-bathing in Martha's garden, are making the most of the heat wave. To be strictly accurate, Eleanor, clad in a brief white bikini and lying on an orange sun-bed is sun-bathing. Martha, dressed in a navy blue one-piece has retired with her deck-chair to the shade of the apple tree. A book rests on her lap, but Martha is not reading. She is miles away, pondering Eleanor's recent revelation, blithely unaware that her friend has a grievance. Not one to brood in silence for long, Eleanor finally speaks:

'There are set formula's for these occasions you know. You are supposed to say; Congratulations Eleanor. I hope you will be very happy.'

Martha mulls over this for a moment or two and then says lightly, 'To be perfectly honest, I was too astonished to say anything. I know you've been seeing this Hank . . . .'

'Luke. You know perfectly well that his name is Luke.'

'Whatever,' she says carelessly. 'I know you've been seeing him for a bit now but when you announced that you were actually going to get formally engaged, I assumed that you were joking.'

' I want to marry him. I know you find it difficult to understand but . . . .'

'Not so long ago you told me that marriage was an outdated ritual.'

'No, Martha. You told me that. I've always kept an open mind on the subject.'

'Yes but you nodded. I remember distinctly. We were on our way back from the Allotment Association Dinner.'

'Well, if I did agree with you once, I've changed my mind now. I love Luke. I know he's a bit eccentric . . . .'

'That's the understatement of the year.'

'Listen who's talking. Don't you think arranging dinner parties for your husband and his mistress, sending her flowers and chocolate, teaching your husband the recorder just the tiniest bit, let's say, unusual?'

'Not really. I have my reasons as you know very well.'

'Be pleased for me, Martha. Luke's a sweet, considerate man. He cares about all the right things: Africa, the environment, badgers, electoral reform. . . .'

'Clog dancing.'

With difficulty, Martha heaves herself out of her deck-chair, looks down on her friend, who is lying on her stomach again and says, 'Your back's done to a turn. Lie in the shade for a bit. I'm going to get myself a cold drink. Do you want one?'

Eleanor rises to her feet and pulls her sun bed into the shade of the apple tree. 'Please.'

After a few minutes, Martha returns with two glasses of lemonade. She hands one to her friend and then sits down again in the deck-chair.

'OK. You win. Congratulations. Satisfied now?'

'Thanks.' Eleanor sips her lemonade gratefully and then tries a more conciliatory tone:

'Luke wants the full set of cutlery: engagement, big wedding, bridesmaids, honeymoon. He's a true romantic. We also want an engagement party.' Martha brightens.

'That's more like it. I like parties.'

'Here, next Friday.'

'Here?'

'Yes. My flat's too small and anyway if the weather is fine we can hold it outside and I haven't got a garden.'

'And you wouldn't want your smart flat messed up.'

'That, too.'

'OK. Have you picked out a ring?'

'No, we are doing that during Luke's lunch break tomorrow, all being well.'

'You mean if he remembers.'

'Luke's at the Scrubs in the morning. He's visiting a client. The man's on remand.'

They drowse in the shade for a while and then Eleanor says sleepily,

'It's OK for Friday then?'

'Fine. We're a bit slack this week as it happens. All we've got is the Choral Society buffet on Tuesday night. All the cold table stuff for that is in the freezer and. . . .'

'What are they singing?'

'*Israel in Egypt*. It's a 'do-it-yourself' *Israel in Egypt*. Anyone can go along and join in.'

'And on Wednesday,' says Eleanor, 'We have the Bonsai Club lunch. What's the name of the little chap who booked it? Bill?'

'Not Bill. Wait . . . Tom. Now what was his other name?'

'Thumb,' grins Eleanor.

'Very funny. Meeks, Tom Meeks,' adding drowsily: 'I wonder if they're all short in the Bonsai Society. Perhaps they bonsai each other.'

Eleanor looks at her watch and then sits up. 'That's me done. What are you doing tomorrow?'

'I'm going up to town. I've got some shopping to do. I

might buy a new dress for your party, and I'm also going to Jeremy's flat to pick up some of his stuff.'

'So he's returned to the nest for the holidays. I thought he was staying in town with his mates.'

'Cheaper at home, unfortunately.'

'Why can't he pick up his own stuff?'

'He's not interested enough, being as it's his files of lecture notes I am collecting. He's got finals next year and he has to get down to some work these holidays. He's too damn idle to pick up the files himself so, being the responsible parent I am, I'm going to do it for him.'

'You shouldn't be running after him, Martha. It's his look out if he fails his exams.'

'You're wrong there. It's ours. If he fails, he won't get a job and that means we will have to continue to keep him.'

When Eleanor gets home she rings Luke. To her surprise he answers the phone immediately.

'It's okay for the party, darling.'

'Good. What party?'

'Our engagement party. I asked Martha this afternoon and she's fine about it. Remember we are having it at her house. Friday, don't forget. And don't ask any of your clients.'

'Friday, next week?'

'No, this week. That's what we decided.'

'Only I'm not sure about this Friday. I thought we decided next week.'

'No we didn't. It was your idea to get engaged and you said you wanted everyone to know and that we should celebrate by having a party and the sooner the better. You went on and on about making a commitment.'

'I know and I do want to make a commitment, till death us do part and all that. The only thing is that the Youth Club are having a barbecue on Friday and I promised . . . .'

'You must tell them you won't be there. Do you understand?'

Monday, late afternoon.

Martha is walking down a street of large semi detached houses off Crough End Broadway, wearing her beige linen 'town suit' and matching heeled sandals and has piled her hair up on top of her head. It has been a long day and, partly because she is weighed down by numerous shopping bags and partly because of the heat, Martha is very tired. She walks slowly, keeping an eye out for the house numbers. Then she spots a large double fronted villa with a cypress tree by the gate. That's the one. The front door is ajar, so she mounts the three steps leading up to it and goes inside. Duncan's flat is on the first floor, she recalls, so she quits the black tiled hallway and mounts the stairs. At the top of the curving stairway is a broad landing and straight ahead of her is Duncan's front door. She marches up to the door and knocks.

'Who is it?' A voice from within.

'Martha Brown.'

There is a longish pause and then a scuffling sound from behind the door.

'Martha who?'

Impatiently: 'Jeremy's mum.'

'He's not here.'

'I know he's not here. Can I come in?'

There is another long pause, then: 'Can I put you on hold for a minute?'

Martha sighs and drops her various bags on the shabby landing carpet. Her feet are aching and she is dying to sit down. She taps one foot impatiently, and then, hearing footsteps mounting the stairs, turns. A tall, dark haired man with an impressive tan, wearing a lightweight, dark blue Italian suit and the kind of craggy good looks you normally only see in films, is striding towards her. He smiles, revealing a row of dazzling white teeth, 'Can't you get in? Here, I'll get the lazy sod out of bed.'

He raps on the door. 'Duncan! It's dad. Let me in.'

The voice from within says, 'Okay, okay, I'm coming. I was just clearing up a bit like you said.' The door opens a crack, 'Has Jeremy's mum gone?'

The good looking man holds out a hand, 'Hallo, Jeremy's mum. I'm Duncan's dad, George Wallis.'

Martha tries very hard to stand straight as she takes the proffered hand, but it is difficult because her knees are buckling, 'Martha, Martha Brown.'

The door to the flat is open now but for a moment neither Duncan's dad nor Martha go through it. Martha is definitely ogling, what did he say his name was? Ah yes, George, and George is also eyeing Martha with some interest. Fortunately, in spite of being hot and tired Martha is looking her best. The tan she has acquired during the heatwave suits her and the sparkle that meeting an attractive new man has given her isn't doing any harm either.

George speaks first: 'I'm staying with Duncan at present, but he hasn't got round to having another key cut as yet. Have you been shopping?'

Martha suddenly remembers what Jeremy told her about Duncan's dad and deflates a little. Oh dear, he's a transvestite. Pity. Then she perks up again. It's not every day you shake hands with a transvestite and even if he is, he's still the most attractive man she's met in years. 'Yes,' she squawks. 'I seem to have bought quite a lot.'

'So you must be exhausted. Come inside and I'll make you a cup of tea, or, if you prefer, something stronger.'

Gathering up her shopping bags, George Wallis leads Martha into a large room, which looks as if it has been in the path of a small size hurricane. There is a low black leather couch as well as various easy chairs, but Martha is at a loss where to sit because every seat is covered with items of clothing, plates, a sleeping bag, towels, a disembowelled pillow, shoes, is that a condom? Yes and there's another. At one end of the room are long windows that overlook the street. Duncan is darting about, gathering up glasses, wine bottles, beer cans, ash trays, plates and piling them up onto a table at the far end of the room. Duncan's dad removes a pair of underpants, a wine bottle and a high-heeled shoe from the sofa and says, 'Sorry about the mess. Normally we are quite civilised. We had a bit of a do last night, as I expect you can see. Do sit down, please. Now what can I get you to drink?'

'Tea, please,' squeaks Martha. *Get a grip*, she tells herself.

'Tea for the lady, Duncan,' says his father, removing a toothbrush, a towel and three cans of beer from an easy chair and then sitting down himself.

Duncan, a younger, but more anxious version of his father is hovering at the door that leads into the kitchen. Now he shoots through it and Martha hears cupboard doors opening and closing and then a crash.

Duncan reappears, 'Sorry, no milk. Sorry, about the . . . I've just broken a cup . . . sorry.'

'Then make some coffee. I expect Martha takes it black anyway. Do stop twittering, boy.'

Duncan looks anxiously towards his friend's mother, 'The mess. Sorry. I meant to get it cleared up but . . . .'

'Do you think Martha has led such a sheltered life that she's never seen the aftermath of a party before? Come on.'

Martha grins: 'I was a student myself once. Many years ago of course.'

Oozing charm, 'Oh not that long ago, surely.'

Martha is more relaxed now. She bats her eyes at Duncan's dad. It's been a long time since she flirted with an attractive man, even if he is a transvestite, but she remembers how it is done.

Duncan is scrabbling about in the kitchen. He returns and says to his father, 'Dad, you had the coffee last.'

George/Duncan's dad/whatever rises in one fluid movement from his chair, 'For God's sake Duncan. If you can't find the coffee give the lady a glass of wine. There's some in the fridge,' and as Duncan disappears into the kitchen, 'I'll have one as well and make sure you wash the glasses first.' He grins quizzically at Martha, 'Wine okay?'

'Fine, fine. You don't have to entertain me you know. All I came for was Jeremy's lecture notes.'

Duncan emerges from the kitchen with two glasses of white wine. He says, 'I think I know where Jeremy's notes are. I'll go and get them for you if you like.'

'Thanks.' Duncan leaves the room and his father puts down his glass and begins to collect up more glasses and plates. Martha hesitates for a moment and then gets up to help him.

'There's no need for you to do that.'

'No trouble.' Martha goes into the kitchen. She piles up crockery and glasses on the draining board, fills the sink with water and starts to wash up. George carries more crockery through from the sitting room and very efficiently begins to restore order to the kitchen. When he has done all he can, he takes a tea cloth and dries the glasses that Martha has washed.

He looks sideways at her as he wipes: 'So you were a bit of a party animal in your time?'

'Martha laughs, 'Still am, given half a chance. In one of those bags resting on your couch is a dress I plan to wear at a party on Friday night. It's an engagement party for a misguided friend.'

George is intrigued: 'Misguided? In what way?'

'Eleanor, my friend, has got it into her head that she wants to marry this guy Luke.'

'Is he that bad?'

'No. He's nice enough, although rather eccentric, but she doesn't have to marry him for God's sake.'

'You're not into marriage then?' Martha can hear the amusement and interest in the man's voice, as she passes him another glass.

She keeps her voice light: 'The concept, yes. In practice, well it's unrealistic. How can you expect two people to live together for years and remain civil to each other, let alone in love.'

'So tell me, are you married?'

Martha is really embarrassed now. She feels her cheeks flushing as she says, 'I am married, as a matter of fact. I married young. That's my only excuse. I said yes before thinking the whole thing through.'

'And you're still living with. . .?'

'Martin, yes.'

George raises his eyebrows quizzically, 'Not divorced then?'

'Not as such, no.'

'As such?' George opens a wall cupboard and begins to put away the clean glasses and crockery. Martha has finished her wine now. She badly needs another one. It seems that George reads her thoughts because he finds another bottle of wine in the fridge and refills her glass. Martha takes a sip and says, 'Martin and I are married, it has to be said.'

George cuts to the chase: 'You don't get on.'

'We get on okay, by and large, on the whole, all things considered. . . .'

'As such.' George looks solemnly at Martha and she begins to laugh. She is determined to put him straight about her marriage though, so she soldiers on: 'Well, the truth is we won't necessarily be married for that much longer, if all goes according to plan.'

'You've met someone else.'

'Not me. Martin. He's met a charming girl, called Jill. There have been a few, well, teething problems with their relationship, but I have every confidence it will all work out in the end.'

George puts down his tea towel.

'Let's leave the rest for Duncan. You've done quite enough. Come and sit down and finish your wine in comfort and tell me more about your fascinating marriage and this girl, Jill.' He guides Martha back into the sitting room where she sits down again on the sofa. This time George sits down beside her.

'You're all for it then: this relationship of your husband. Is the party on Friday for him and his intended?'

'No. I told you it was for my friend Eleanor and her intended.'

'Sorry, I must have lost focus for a moment.'

Martha hesitates and then takes the plunge: 'Do come. To the party, I mean. Bring Duncan, or a friend . . . whatever.'

'Wild horses won't keep me away,' he is murmuring when his son, carrying a file, re-enters the room. Duncan hands Martha the file. She looks at it in disbelief:

'Is that all? He's been studying for three years; surely, there must be more than this.'

Duncan smiles nervously. 'Jeremy writes small,' he says.

Tuesday evening
Luke, Jill and a fat, cross-looking girl are sitting at a table outside The Bull, a pub near the community hall where the recorder orchestra rehearses. The three have just attended an extra rehearsal because a concert is looming. Normally they rehearse on Monday nights. The weather still continues fine and warm so most of the pub customers have elected to sit at tables in the pub gardens. Luke, Jill and the fat girl are seated under an old beech tree, Luke and the fat girl drinking lager, and Jill sipping

a glass of white wine. Soft green light filters through the branches. The fat girl looks furtively round the other tables, then rolls herself a cigarette. She does not want to be here at this poncy pub and is looking for an opportunity to leave. When Luke takes out his descant from a pocket she decides to delay her departure no longer,

'I've gotta go,' she says.

Luke puts the recorder back into his pocket and pats the girl's hand. Her finger nails are black and her hands a greyish colour. 'Finish your drink first.' Then turning to Jill he explains, 'She's terrified her mates will see her. Not cool this pub.' He gestures to the well-heeled, chattering customers. 'Too middle class.' He looks at the girl again. She is peering through a tangle of unwashed hair into her glass. Jill eyes her nervously. She's never sat at a table with someone in back leathers before.

'You're safe enough here. None of your gang would be seen dead in this place, Melody.'

The girl gasps, 'I've told yer and told yer not to call me that. Me name's Shaz.' Jill smiles politely and Luke continues, 'Shaz is a client of mine. Her real name is Mel. . . .'

'Leave it out will yer?'

Jill leans towards the girl: 'I understand. Street cred's crucial.'

Shaz nods and takes a gulp of her lager. Jill examines her bent head. She is not sure but she thinks she can see something move.

'You must enjoy playing though. You come every week without fail to recorder orchestra and now this extra rehearsal. I mean it's not cool is it? The recorder.'

Shaz shrugs. 'S'alright. 'Is idea,' she says, pointing to Luke. 'Part of me community service. It's supposed to keep me off the streets.'

'But you play so well.'

'Not as well as Norman.'

'Norman who plays bass?'

She gestures towards Luke. 'Yeah. Old Norman's another of 'is clients. Norman was a flasher before he joined the recorder orchestra.'

'A high class flasher though,' said Luke. 'He used to flash to the queues of concert goers outside the Albert Hall and was well known at Covent Garden.'

'Shaz rambles on, 'I learnt to play at primary school. Now I play bass guitar as well and a bit of sax. Anyway as I say, I gotta go.'

'Well I think it's just lovely that you come along every week.'

Luke grins. 'It's not as though I twist your arm or anything is it Shaz?'

The girl gets up. Luke is writing on a piece of paper.

'Me and my girl friend are having a party on Friday night. I've written down the address. Bring a friend and Shaz, only wash first.'

Jill glances over his shoulder at the paper.

'That's the Brown's address.'

'That's where we are holding the party,' says Luke and hands the paper to Shaz. She shambles off.

Jill turns back to Luke, 'About this Norman, the flasher . . . .'

'He's a brilliant player. '

Before Jill can question Luke any further, she spots Jeremy threading his way through the tables towards them. Then, with a sinking heart, she sees who is behind him. It is Lucinda and following her is a stout middle-aged man with protruding eyes. Luke also sees the trio advancing so he pulls up three extra chairs. Lucinda has spotted Jill, but there's nothing she can do about it without making a scene so she finds herself sitting at the same table as the bitch who seduced her father. Ignoring

Jill, she introduces Manfred to Luke.

'You must be the recorder player,' says Manfred gripping Luke's hand so tightly that he winces.

'Have you got a problem with that?' Luke is wondering if he will ever play the recorder again.

Manfred continues the attack: 'I played the recorder when I was child. Toy instrument isn't it?'

'If you say so,' replies Luke so gently that Manfred is abashed. That is, as abashed as a brass player can be.

'What are you having?'

'Perrier water,' says Lucinda choosing the chair most distant from Jill.

'I'll have a pint, thanks,' says Manfred.

'He'll have a half,' says Lucinda.

'I'll have a half.'

'Hello beautiful.' Jeremy abandons his sister and her aggressive boyfriend and sits down next to Jill. 'A pint for me.' Then he rises again. 'Here, I'll give you a hand.'

The three men go off to the bar to get the drinks. Lucinda stares pointedly after the men.

Finally she hears a quiet, 'I'm Jill Peters.'

'I know who you are, the bitch that had an affair with my father.'

'Martha doesn't mind.'

'How dare you call my mother, Martha?'

'It's her name. She told me to call her Martha. We're friends, good friends.'

'You are not my mother's friend.'

Hostilities cease at this point because the men return with the drinks. As he sits down on the other side of Jill, Luke makes an announcement:

'Ladies, I was just saying to the fellas here that me and Eleanor are having a party on Friday and you are all invited.' He looks at them both expectantly. 'Jill?'

'I'd love to come.'

'Jeremy?'

' I doubt I'd be able to get out of it even if I wanted to, being as it is at our house.'

'Lucinda? Manfred isn't quite sure. You'll have to persuade him.'

Lucinda says sharply, 'Of course we'll come. I'll need to be there to give mummy a hand.' She looks accusingly at her boyfriend, who finishes off his half lager in one gulp and looking longingly in the direction of the bar says, 'I was a bit doubtful when Luke first mentioned the party because I've got a gig on Friday, but it should be over by ten. I'll come along after that, if it's all right with you, Luke.'

Lucinda is seething and looks round for someone on whom she can vent her spleen. Manfred is the obvious choice.

'Gig? What gig? You never told me you had a gig on Friday.'

'I did. I told you this morning, but you were so busy telling me off for leaving the lavatory seat up that you weren't listening.'

Wednesday morning

Martha is in her kitchen checking through the food for the Bonsai Society lunch, all arranged in trays on the kitchen table, when there is a knock at the door. She opens it and finds Tom, the secretary of the society, outside. He is a Hobbit sized man with a shining bald head and a smile that stretches from ear to ear. Bicycle clips secure his grey flannel trousers bottoms and he is clutching a flat cap in his hands. He looks as though he has just escaped from a black and white film set in the industrial north.

'Hello Tom, come in. I wasn't expecting to see you until later.'

The small man enters the kitchen, but remains hovering nervously by the door. When he speaks he has a thick Yorkshire accent: 'I thought I'd just come round and settle up like.'

Before Martha can reply there is another knock on the door and the rugby club captain enters the kitchen. He towers over Tom. 'Hi Tom. How you doing?' And punches him playfully on the arm. The small man totters but quickly recovers and punches the rugby captain back. He has to reach up to do it though and still only manages to connect with the captain's stomach.

'Hi Nige. Coming to the lunch?'

'Nothing would keep me away. I've sampled some of this lady's delicious food before.' Then, turning to Martha, he added, 'I've come to pay my bill. Sorry, I know it's a bit overdue. Look, I've written a cheque. Is that okay?'

Martha pockets the cheque and writes a receipt, 'I didn't know you were a member of the Bonsai Society. You're too t. . .I mean I didn't think you'd have much time for gardening.'

Tom signs his cheque with a flourish and says, 'Nigel's one of our keenest members. He's even been to Japan. That's how keen he is.'

The rugby captain looks round hopefully: 'Your pretty friend not here today?'

'Ah,' simpers Martha coyly. 'You were hoping to see Eleanor? Tell you what, there's going to be a party here on Friday and Eleanor's coming, in fact she and . . .is the star guest. Why don't you come along? Why don't you both come?'

ELEVEN

Thursday night

Martin is riffling through the clothes in his cupboard and has thrown six or seven shirts onto the bed with a tangle of ties. Suddenly dissatisfied with his entire wardrobe, he stamps out on the landing in his underpants.

'Martha? Martha?' There is no reply. 'Martha!'

From below: 'I'm busy Martin. I'm still cooking.'

'I need your help.' He returns to the bedroom and continues to ransack his wardrobe. Finally, Martha, wearing her butcher's apron over her jeans, enters the room.

'Look Martha I've got nothing to wear tomorrow night.' Martin picks a bright red shirt from the bed and puts it against himself and then selects a black and green striped tie.

Martha shakes her head decisively: 'No.'

Martin puts the shirt and tie back on the bed and picks out a pair of grey slacks. 'What do you think? Understated but sophisticated?' He chooses a blue shirt.

'Stay with the blue.' Martha is not very interested. 'Sorry Martin but I've got to go and get on. There's still heaps to do.'

Martin is hurt. 'I thought you would want me to look smart, being as Jill's coming. Perhaps I ought to buy . . . .'

Incredibly, Martha suddenly realises she has completely forgotten to invite Jill to the party. What with going up to London, the excitement of meeting Duncan's dad and all the preparations for the party, Martha's plans for the reunion of Martin and Jill have gone completely from her mind. She's annoyed.

'I didn't know Jill was coming. Who invited Jill? Did you?'

'No, Luke asked her if you must know.'

'Why didn't you tell me she was coming?'

'I'm telling you now.' He looks more closely at his wife. 'You're miffed aren't you?'

'No.'

'You're jealous.'

'Don't be ridiculous.'

Suddenly the light dawns. 'You're annoyed because you didn't invite Jill yourself. It's fine Jill and I seeing each other but only as long as Martha masterminds the arrangements.'

Martin has hit the bull's eye, but it isn't in Martha to admit it. Instead she says, 'Look, somehow I'll find time tomorrow morning to buy you a shirt that will go beautifully with those understated but sophisticated trousers.'

She thinks she has scored but she hasn't. Martin is still looking infuriatingly smug, as Martha leaves the bedroom and heads back to the kitchen.

Friday night

It is a warm summer's evening and the light from the evening sun streams through the windows of the Brown's kitchen. The scent of honeysuckle and newly mown grass drifts in but Eleanor, Martha and Martin are too busy to notice. Martin is setting up a bar on the kitchen table. Martha is in the dining room arranging the buffet on the dining room table. Eleanor brings through the last two quiches and the food preparation is complete.

Martin has finished arranging the 'bar' now. He begins to leave the kitchen.

'Where are you going?'

'He produces his instructions list and reads: 'Do bar. Done that. Put out nuts, crisps etc. Done that. Put out chairs in the garden. That's what I'm up to.'

'And get the camping tables out of the shed and the lights.'

'I know, I know. It's all in hand.'

'Just checking. Did you use those little Chinese bowls that are in the dining room cupboard for the . . . .'

Martin heads for the garden, calling smugly over his shoulder.. 'Of course.'

Martha pulls a stool out from under 'the bar' and sits down.

'I think we're just about ready. By the way I've invited Nigel.' She looks pointedly at Eleanor, who is examining her nails.

'Ask me who Nigel is.'

'OK, if it will make you happy. Who is Nigel?'

'The rugby club captain, and he fancies you rotten.'

'Don't start your match-making tricks on me, Martha. Please.'

'Would I do that?'

'Yes and don't. I'm spoken for.'

'Well there's only one thing to say to that: where is he?'

'He'll be here.'

There is the sound of the door bell.

Martha says, 'We're on. I'll get it.'

'No you won't. You can't answer the door looking like that.' Martha is wearing her butcher's apron over shorts and a murky top. 'Go up and change. I'll get it.'

Much later, the same night

The party is in full swing. In the kitchen there's a crowd of people helping themselves to drinks from the 'bar'. More guests are filling their plates with food in the dining room. In the sitting room, where the lights have been turned down low and the furniture pushed back, couples are dancing. The French windows that lead from the sitting room into the garden are flung wide and more guests are dancing on the lawn and others standing around in groups chattering.

One of these groups is made up of members of the recorder

orchestra. They have seated themselves round one of Martha and Martin's camping tables. Three of the women are wearing tie-dye tops and two of the men sport beards. Sitting between two tie-dye tops is Norman, the erstwhile flasher, dressed in a pair of grey flannel trousers and an open-neck blue and white check shirt. Norman is not happy. He is hot, his head is glistening with sweat, he is ill at ease and wishes he had not come. Tentatively he fingers the top of his zip. Faith, the woman on his right slaps his hand away.

Opposite to Norman sits a man wearing a sharp Gucci suit. This is Jasper and he also wishes that he had not come to the party. He is bored and looking for a chance to escape his fellow players.

Jill, who is dancing on the lawn with Martin, looks anxiously towards the group. She is wearing a very short white frock which leaves her shoulders and a lot of cleavage bare, long drop ear rings and high, white, backless sandals.

'Do you think I should go over and break them up?'

'No darling,' murmurs Martin who is wearing a short-sleeved navy shirt with his understated slacks. Having sampled a few glasses of the claret cup, Martin is feeling mellow. He gently caresses Jill's smooth young skin, secretly delighted that his neighbours can see him monopolising the company of this attractive young woman.

Meanwhile, Jasper has spotted Lucinda standing next to a stout middle-aged man on the patio. Lucinda is gazing up at the man, her flower like face – that's how Jasper sees it – tilted upwards, showing off her long slender neck. She appears totally absorbed in whatever the fatuous idiot is saying. Gazing longingly at the young woman, Jasper decides that she must be a quiet, contemplative sort of girl – his sort of girl. He makes a vow that, at some point during the evening, he will make an opportunity to speak to her.

Lucinda is looking contemplative because she's working out exactly what she is going to say to Manfred, when he finally shows his fucking face. Lucinda is not listening to a word the stout man utters. Just to set the record straight, he is describing in minute detail how, by taking a new route to work, he's managed to cut off a whole minute from the journey time. So she's not missed anything.

Jeremy is dancing with Eleanor, but both are distracted. Eleanor because Luke has failed to materialise and Jeremy, because he is watching his father dance with Jill.

Meanwhile, Martha is in the hall welcoming Duncan, his dad, the rugby club captain and Tom Meeks from the Bonsai Society who have all arrived at the same time. Smiling with relief – she was just beginning to think that George was not going to show – she introduces Nigel, the rugby captain and Tom to Duncan and his father and then leads them to the bar.

'Help yourselves.'

Nigel is looking round hopefully.

Martha smiles at him: 'You'll find Eleanor in the garden. She's dancing with Jeremy.'

Duncan brightens up. 'I'll take a beer out to him. Coming, Tom?'

He collects three cans of lager from the 'bar' and heads out of the kitchen door and into the garden with Tom trotting after him. Nigel follows more slowly.

Duncan's dad, to Martha's disappointment, is not in drag. But he is looking very sexy anyway, dressed in well cut cream trousers and a black silk shirt.

'You look ravishing,' he says. And she does. Her new plum coloured dress shows off her curvaceous figure to great advantage and matches her lipstick exactly. The lipstick was applied by and belongs to Eleanor. In fact Eleanor applied all Martha's makeup and also arranged her hair on top of her head.

George – Martha tells herself she must stop calling him Duncan's dad – now reaches up, captures an escaped curl and tucks it back behind her ear.

'I can hear one of my old favourites. Let's dance.' He leads her into the sitting room, where only two other couples are dancing and draws her close.

Nigel is dancing with Eleanor. He nuzzles her neck. 'Happy birthday,' he murmurs. She draws away.

'It's not my birthday.'

Puzzled, Nigel peers into his partner's face. Christ, she is even more attractive than he remembered. 'Sorry. I'm sure Martha told me that this party was in your honour.'

'It is.'

'So?'

'It's my engagement party, actually.'

'Then . . . where is he?' he says, looking around.

'He's not here yet,' says Eleanor. 'I expect him any minute.'

Nigel moves in closer and whispers, 'Well . . . in the meantime . . .'

Martin and Jill have returned to the sitting room. They have settled themselves down on the sofa, Jill snuggled against Martin's shoulder. Martin is moodily watching his wife dance with a tall stranger. Does she have to dance so close? George is also watching Martin – and Jill.

'So the fella on the sofa is your husband? Martin – as such.'

'And the girl is Jill, the one I told you about. She's very attractive. Don't you think?'

'She's pretty enough in a vacuous sort of way.'

They dance for a moment in silence and then George says, 'Your husband must be stupid.'

'Martin is not stupid.'

'He must be to dump a clever, witty, attractive woman for a girl. You, my dear Martha, are everything a man could desire.

112

Everything this man desires, at any rate.'

Martha giggles and points to a fair-haired young man – one of Jeremy's old school friends – who has just entered the room: 'Come on, George. He's more your type surely. Something tells me my virtue is quite safe with you.'

George laughs so loudly at this, that he wakes up one of the Breman's neighbours who has fallen asleep in an easy chair by the window. Martin, who is also nodding off – to Jill's annoyance – comes to with a start. He glares at George. So what does he find so funny all of a sudden?

'If you think your virtue is safe with me, my sweet girl, then you couldn't be more wrong. Don't you know that ever since I entered the house I've been plotting how to get you into bed.'

Martha can feel a flush spreading up from her neck into her face: 'But Jeremy said . . . .'

'That I was a transvestite. Look, sometimes I enjoy cross-dressing. That's all there is to it. Every now and again, when the mood takes me I dress as a woman.'

'Why?'

'Because I get some kind of kick out of it I suppose. But that does not mean I fancy other men. On the contrary.'

'But I thought . . .'

'Most people do.'

'Your wife . . . .'

'Is a bitch of the first order but she threw me out because I borrowed one of her frocks. It was much too small and I split it down the back. Anyway the marriage was already on its last legs. Neither of us was sorry when it finally turned up its toes and died.'

'I see,' murmured Martha, not quite sure what to think about all this.

'I'm glad we've sorted all that out,' George says softly. 'And you're still dancing with me, so all hope's not lost.' They dance in silence for a moment or two, then Martha laughs and says, 'I was disappointed that you didn't come in drag though. A man in drag would have given so much cachet to my party.'

George pretends to be affronted. 'Let me tell you that if I had come to this do in drag, no one would have known. When I dress as a woman I make sure that no one has the slightest inkling that I am a man.'

'I don't believe it. You can always tell.'

George shrugs. 'I don't have the gear any more and anyway I'm living at Duncan's flat now. Anyway she burnt all my stuff. If I'd had the dress you're wearing now hanging in my wardrobe, I might have been tempted though. It's stunning.'

To her astonishment Martha hears her voice saying, 'Would you like to try it on?'

'Now? Here?'

'Well, we'd have to go upstairs of course.'

She can't believe she said that.

'Yes, we would wouldn't we?'

The music stops and the couple stand isolated in the middle of the floor.

George decides to play it light, 'You don't mean that.' There is a hint of challenge in his voice. Enough to make Martha feel that there's no going back now.

'I do. I've got all the gear upstairs. I've even got a wig somewhere. I bet that if you get yourself done up as a woman, then come down stairs and show yourself, you won't be able to convince anyone that you are the genuine article.'

'How much do you bet?'

'A tenner.'

'You're on.'

'Come on then.' Martha follows George out of the room.

Fortunately Martin does not see the dark-haired man leading

his wife upstairs. This is because immediately the music stops, Jill sends him into the kitchen to fetch her a drink. In the kitchen Martin gets chatting to a neighbour who is also a member of his golf club. He gets so engrossed in the chat with his friend that for a time Martin completely forgets that Jill is still on the sofa awaiting his return. As the minutes tick by Jill becomes more and more annoyed. Thus, when Jeremy strolls into the room and comes over to ask her to dance, she agrees without any argument. Martin's been a bit distant all evening and now he's left her stranded without so much as a word. It will do him a power of good to return to the room and find her gone. She follows Jeremy into the garden.

It's a warm evening and many guests have drifted outside. Among them is Lucinda who is dancing with Duncan. Duncan has always had a soft spot for his friend's sister and he thinks she looks even more stunning than usual tonight in her flimsy pink dress. Now that Duncan's got to hold Lucinda in his arms, things couldn't be going better. The pretty girl seems absolutely fascinated by everything he has to say. Her large blue eyes never leave his face. Duncan first explains the off side trap. Then he goes on to describe how he scored the best goal of the season in the final minutes of his last match, using the strategy he had just so minutely described.

Of course, Lucinda is not listening to a word. Inside Lucinda is a coiled spring of rage. Yes, she tells herself, a coiled spring of rage. And she can't wait to unleash it on that fucking horn player. She'll tell him to stick that French Horn where the sun don't shine, when eventually he shows his fucking face.

Then her reverie is interrupted. One of the recorder players – the well dressed good looking one – detaches himself from the group and cuts in on Lucinda and her partner. Duncan is so mortified at the sheer gall of the man that he relinquishes her without protest. Lucinda doesn't argue. This chap is quite attractive and she adores the masterful way he carries her off. Snuggling her head against her new partner's shoulder, for a moment she forgets her coiled spring of rage. Jasper is so astonished by his own audacity – this isn't his normal style at all – that now he is at a loss for words. Lucinda waits for her tall dark handsome abductor (that's how tomorrow she will describe him on the telephone to her best friend) to introduce himself but when he doesn't she decides to take the initiative.

'I'm Lucinda,' she says, switching on her most dazzling smile. It has the desired effect. Tall, dark and handsome gulps and then mutters so quietly that she has to lean closer, which is not easy considering that at the moment it would be difficult to fit a spatula between them.

'Jasper – sorry about that – my mother's idea.'

'I like the name. It's cool.'

'I've been wanting to talk to you all evening. I hope you didn't mind me cutting in like that.'

Lucinda looks up through her lashes and is pleased with what she sees: deep-set, deep-brown eyes, a patrician nose and an admiring smile.

'No, Duncan's just a friend of my brother, Jeremy.'

'So you didn't come with anybody?'

Lucinda is a girl of principles and although she is furious with Manfred and will probably dump him quite soon, she is still at this point in time, she tells herself, spoken for.

'My partner's not arrived yet. He's a French Horn player and he's got a gig tonight.'

Over Lucinda's shoulder Jasper espies a burly figure, dressed in an evening suit and bow tie – every inch a brass player – peering out of the French windows.

'Is that him?'

Manfred is not a pretty sight. His face is red and glistening, his eyes staring and his bow tie has lodged itself beneath one ear. As he tries to negotiate the step which leads down onto the patio, Manfred trips, crashes into a flower-pot and finally connects with the ground. He lands flat on his back, his head resting on a hummock of soil.

The coil of rage inside Lucinda unfurls. She abandons her partner, marches over to her prostrate love and stands, hands on hips, glaring down at him positively pulsating with anger.

'Where have you been? I said WHERE HAVE YOU BEEN? You PROMISED me you'd be here just after ten and it's now GONE ONE. MANFRED ARE YOU LISTENING?'

Manfred makes no attempt to rise from his prone position among the ruins of broken flower pot, soil and uprooted plants. His eyes are closed so for a moment the still incandescent Lucinda thinks he has passed out. This is not the case. Manfred opens first one bloodshot eye and then the other. At last, smiling lovingly he burbles, 'Hello darling.'

Lucinda is paralysed by indecision. Which bit of the drunken imbecile should she kick first? 'Manfred!'

'Florian . . . .' He brings out the word triumphantly. 'First thrumpet . . . marvellous player . . . marvellous chap . . . marvellissimo. We went to this . . . went for a few drinks. Luce?'

Lucinda takes a step backwards, to give herself plenty of room, but the gods decide to rescue Manfred just this once for as she is about to raise her foot, Lucinda feels two arms encircle her waist. She is spun round and finds herself facing the handsome Jasper.

'Leave him Lucinda. You were dancing with me, remember?'

Lucinda allows herself to be led away.

God, she looks lovely when she's angry, thinks Manfred as he sinks into oblivion.

Upstairs in Martha and Martin's bedroom, George is

seated in front of Martha's dressing table mirror. He is wearing Martha's dress. The zip won't do up and it's rather short, but from the front it looks fine. Martha has placed a black wig on his head and pulled the front hair down into a fringe. Most of his face is made up: thick eye-liner and mascara, pan foundation and lots of blusher – and he is about to apply a plumy red lipstick. In the dimly lit room – only the lamps either side of the bed are switched on – George makes a fairly convincing if tarty woman. Martha, the real thing in a cream silk dressing gown, is standing behind him admiring their joint handiwork.

'A kiss please before I apply the lipstick.' Martha leans over and kisses him. It's clear from the kiss that things have moved on since the pair mounted the stairs together. Not too far though. The bed is undisturbed.

Martha finds George very attractive and she is very tempted, but she does draw the line at having sex with this new man in the marital bed. At the end of the kiss, he turns back to the mirror and applies the lipstick. Then he looks questioningly at Martha's reflection in the mirror.

'What do you think?'

'You look gorgeous.'

'So do you and I hope you are appreciating my restraint.' He blots his lipstick.

'I am. Now the shoes.' She produces a pair of black sandals. They are much too small.

'Martha! The Freemans are just leaving. Where are you Martha?' It is Eleanor's voice. In a panic Martha drags on a pair of trousers and a black top from the chair.'

'Hang on. I'm coming.' There's the sound of steps on the stairs. Martha gets to the door before Eleanor reaches it and disappears through it.

Meanwhile, Martin, finding Jill has deserted him, has wandered out into the garden. He sees that she is dancing with his son. He looks round. Where's Martha? The last time he saw her she was dancing with that tall, sinister-looking chap. Martha, in fact, is standing on the front porch waving off the Freemans.

Martin goes back into the sitting room, where a few people are still dancing, then the dining room, where many dirty plates and glasses but little food is left and finally to the kitchen. Eleanor and Nigel are kissing by the sink and a very small man is making himself a cheese sandwich at the kitchen table. No Martha. She must be upstairs. He mounts the stairs and enters his bedroom. He sees a figure sitting at the dressing table and at first thinks it is Martha because the woman is wearing the same coloured dress as his wife. As he advances further into the room, however, he sees that it is a dark haired woman, who is very heavily made up. Quite an attractive woman though. Funny that he has not noticed her before this evening.

'Hallo,' he says. 'I don't think we've met. Are you a friend of Eleanor's?'

'The strange woman has a very low, sexy voice. Martin moves closer.

'No, of Martha's. I hope you don't mind me being in your bedroom, but Martha said it would be all right.'

'Feel free to come into my bedroom anytime.' Martin is delighted with this line. Like just about everyone else at the party, he is rather drunk.

The woman turns and looks at him from under her lashes, 'And you must be Martin. Martha's told me so much about you.'

Martin is surprised. He sits down heavily on the bed and says, 'Well, there you have the advantage. She's told me nothing about you.'

George gets up from the dressing table and goes to sit next to Martin on the bed. Who says he can't pass as a woman?

George moves closer. He's not going to score with Martha tonight, but her husband seems a distinct possibility.

He lifts a lock of hair: 'I wonder if you could help me. Can you see? My ear-ring has got entangled. Can you fix it for me?'

Jill sees Martin go back into the house and after a moment's thought, decides she has been a bit mean leaving him like that, so she makes her excuses to the hurt Jeremy and goes into the house to look for him. Only she can't find him. Perhaps he's gone upstairs. She mounts the stairs. Martha, returning to the hall after waving off the departing guests, sees Jill's retreating back. Good. She can introduce George to her husband's mistress. Let's see if she is deceived.

Now everything happens very quickly. Jill opens the bedroom door as Martin reaches forward to disentangle this strange woman's ear-ring. As he moves, George seizes Martin's wrist and pulls them both back onto the pillows. Caught off balance, Martin collapses on top of George just as Jill enters the room. Martin hears the footsteps and rolls over in time to see the shocked face of his ex-mistress. Before he can say a word, she runs out of the room. He turns back to Georgina, who he can now see is a George because the chap's wig has fallen onto the pillow.

'Shit.' says George

Martha reaches the top of the stairs at exactly the same time as Jill. 'Jill!' she calls, but the girl continues on her way downstairs. Martha enters the bedroom and finds Martin and George sitting side by side on the bed.

'Shit,' says Martha.

Later – or early next day – it depends how you look at it, Martha, Jeremy, Martin and Eleanor are gathered in the kitchen drinking coffee. They are all exhausted because, at Martha's insistence, they have just finished clearing up.

'Great party,' says Jeremy, 'though I missed the end. By the time I got back from taking Jill home,' he pauses to give a secret smile, 'everyone had gone.'

'I didn't know you'd taken Jill home, Jeremy,' says Martha. 'The last time I saw her was when she came dashing downstairs from the bathroom. She looked a bit upset. '

'She was upset. As soon as she got downstairs, she asked me to take her home. She refused to tell me why.'

'I think she was upset because she found me on the bed with Duncan's dad,' says Martin grimly. 'He was wearing your dress Martha. Why did you let him borrow your dress?'

Actually, Martin is relieved. He considers that he has nothing to fear from Duncan's dad, after all. Any chap that puts on make-up and a long red frock and then makes a pass at her husband is hardly likely to try it on with a chap's wife.

'It's a long story and quite frankly I'm too tired to go into it right now,' says Martha. Eleanor, staring glumly into her coffee, takes no part in this discussion.

Martin says gently, 'You're a bit quiet, El. You should be pleased that your party went so well.'

'It did but there was one essential ingredient to the party missing,' says Eleanor bitterly

'And what was that then?'

'Luke,' says Eleanor. 'Mind if I sleep what's left of the night in Lucinda's room?'

'It will have to be the couch,' Martha says. 'Lucinda's asleep in her bedroom. She's left Manfred again.'

TWELVE

September. Sunday evening

It is early in September.   Martha is having a romantic dinner with George at a four star restaurant off the M25. Jeremy is drinking at a pub nearer home with his friend Duncan, and Lucinda is walking hand in hand with Jasper. They are on their way home from a chamber music concert. Needless to say, Lucinda did not enjoy a single note. 'Another bloody musician,' she is thinking bitterly, as they reach the road where she lives 'I need my head examined.'

All is peace at the Breman house, mainly because Martin is the only member of the family at home. He is upstairs working on his computer, designing a programme that will streamline the client database of his company. Totally focussed, Martin Breman is a happy man.

He is so absorbed that he fails to hear the front door open downstairs. Neither does he register the sound of footsteps – the footsteps of Duncan and Jeremy. He is only roused from his abstraction by the sound of his son's voice calling from the bottom of the stairs.

'Dad, dad, are you still up there, dad?   Is it okay if Duncan stays the night?'

'Fine.'

'Where's the camp bed and the sleeping bags?'

'Ask your mum.' An automatic response that does not require a connection between brain and vocal chords.

'She's out.'

Jeremy returns to the living room where he finds Duncan reclining on the sofa with his feet up.

'I can sleep here. It's very comfortable.'

Exhausted by all that effort Jeremy sinks into an armchair

and picks up the sports section of the Sunday paper.

'Lucinda in?' Duncan asks hopefully.

'She's out with her new bloke. He came to pick her up earlier.'

'She's not with the trumpet player then?

'Horn player. No, unfortunately. She's moved back home again.'

Duncan isn't really listening. 'She's a beautiful girl,' he murmurs wistfully.

Jeremy snorts. He's her brother and knows better.

'You don't know her. You don't have to live with her.'

Duncan is awakened from a brief doze by the entrance of Lucinda, right on cue.

She sweeps into the room wearing a calf length, dark blue skirt and a long-sleeved, cream silk shirt. Draped elegantly round her shoulders is a cashmere cardigan. She ignores her brother and says to Duncan, 'Do you want a drink? I'm going to make myself a cup of camomile tea. Would you like me to make you one?' Without waiting for a reply, Lucinda stalks out of the room.

Delighted, Duncan follows her into the kitchen. 'I've never had camomile tea before,' he confides as she fills the kettle and takes down two mugs from their hooks. She does not reply so he perches nervously on the edge of a chair and says nervously, 'So you are no longer with the trumpet player.'

'Horn player. I'm seeing another chap now and in some ways he's just as bad as Manfred.'

'Another professional musician?'

'No. Jasper does something clever in the city but he plays in the same recorder group as Luke, Eleanor's ex. He collects the boring CD's, goes to concerts all the time and talks about nothing else but music. It's really getting me down.'

'I can see that it would,' says Duncan sympathetically. He

sips the tea enthusiastically, but Lucinda is not paying him much attention. She's still brooding about her new boyfriend.

'Jasper's marvellous looking of course. And he drives a Porche. He adores me of course.'

'I'm not surprised,' he says, wistfully.

'That's the good news. The bad news is that, although I've only been going out with him for three weeks, we've already been to one symphony concert, a performance of ancient music with authentic instruments and an evening of madrigals. To add insult to injury, he expects me to go to his wretched recorder orchestra concert in October. There's only so much a girl can take.'

'Doesn't he ever ask what you want to do?'

'No,' she mutters bitterly. 'He just assumes that I am as obsessed as he is. He says that a person who does not love music is lacking a soul. I have a soul Duncan. It's just that my soul is not interested in classical music.'

'Of course you have a soul, Lucinda,' Duncan says earnestly and very sincerely.

'You have a beautiful soul. I can see your soul. It shines out from your eyes.'

For the first time, Lucinda really looks at her brother's friend and she likes what she sees. She notes the square, manly jawline, the thin noble nose, the way his hair curls a bit either side of each ear and she particularly appreciates the dog-like devotion in his eyes.

'Do you like classical music, Duncan?' she asks.

'No, not at all. I've never understood what all the fuss is about. I'm tone deaf as a matter of fact.'

Lucinda smiles. For a moment Duncan sees nothing but her large, limpid blue eyes. He can feel his heart melting.

'So am I,' she says.

Monday

Monday evening, 7.30 pm prompt, twenty-five players of the recorder orchestra assemble in the community hall. Black plastic chairs are stacked against two white-washed walls, a battered upright piano rests against the third and a low platform projects from the fourth.

The recorder players are a mixed bunch, their ages ranging from Shaz, who is fifteen to Felix who is seventy-six. They are arranged, one stand per pair, in a loose semi-circle in front of their conductor. The rehearsal is just about to start and Bridget, the group's conductor, is handing out parts for the Capriol Suite, one of the pieces the players are preparing for their October concert. Bridget, once a raven-haired colleen, is an Irish woman in her mid-fifties, and has now gone to seed. She is wearing a purple-fringed skirt and an embroidered waistcoat over a white peasant blouse. Her long, coarse hair falls in Medusa like snakes down her back. Bridget wears her hair hanging in this way because she believes that the tangled hair signals the fact that she is a free spirit. Whether she is a free spirit or not is debatable but one thing is quite certain: there is none of the free spirit in either her rehearsal technique or her conducting. Now, because she has lost a vital treble part, she is upset.

'Miriam? Felix? Did you take your treble parts home last week?' She speaks with a marked, Northern Ireland accent.

Miriam, an elderly woman with grey speckled frizzy hair, deep in conversation with Felix a thin man with a long cadaverous face and heavy rimmed spectacles, looks up and says briskly, 'No.'

Jill who shares a stand with Shaz says quickly, 'We haven't got it.'

She turns back to Luke who is playing second tenor and sitting to her right.

'Well, I just can't understand Eleanor's attitude. I would have expected that once you had told her why you weren't able to turn up for the party, she would have understood. I can't believe she dumped you, when you were only doing your job. I mean what choice did you have?'

Shaz decides it's time Jill heard her point of view.

'I didn't ask him to come looking for me in Brighton. It was the last thing I wanted. How do you think I felt when he turned up at that squat in the middle of the night?'

'I know Shaz, but you've got to understand that Luke is responsible for your welfare. He had no choice but to act as he did.'

'What I want to know is why he has to drag the fuzz along with 'im.'

Luke sighs. 'You're fifteen, Shaz, and, according to the law, still in need of care and protection.'

'Is this what you are looking for Bridget?' Norman, who is playing contra-bass, waves the missing part. Bridget snatches the music away from the small man and hands it to Felix.

'All right, everyone. We'll start from the top with the Basse-Danse. Kyle,' she says to a pretty twenty-two year old descant player, who is still chattering to her partner, 'Are you ready? With repeats. And . . . .' At last they are away.

All goes well until they reach the Tordion, the most difficult piece so far. Last week they made a mess of it, according to Bridget. Now they all wait nervously for her to give the signal to start.

'Six-four everyone. Con moto leggerissimo,' drawing out the Italian in a voice that sets Jill's teeth on edge. She nudges Shaz, who crosses her eyes.

'Lightly. Piano, pianissimo.' Then in a more business like tone: 'At letter C, I want Jill to play sop.'

'I know, I know. You told me weeks ago,' mutters Jill.

'Are you ready? I shall give you two for nothing.'

When the orchestra reaches the double bar, it's back to the beginning again. Bridget is still not happy. The descants are sharp. The tenors are flat. The trebles are rushing ahead, especially fifth bar of A and the basses are dragging behind. The ensemble is poor.

'You are just not together. You are not watching me.'

She takes them through A twice, B once and C three times. Finally she is satisfied and calls out, 'Take a break everyone. Fifteen minutes.'

Luke and Jill leave their stands and wander out into the vestibule for a breath of air. It is very hot in the main hall. For a moment or two neither speaks. Luke is subdued, Jill notices. He is not his usual bouncy self and he is looking even more scruffy than usual. His granddad shirt has stains down the front, his feet (in open sandals) look grubby, his beard needs a trim.

'Did you explain to Eleanor about how you had to go after Shaz?' she asks at last.

Luke looks at the young woman in surprise.

'Yes I did explain to Eleanor exactly what had happened and I went to see her again this week to try to explain again, but she just isn't interested any more. Why should a beautiful woman like Eleanor hang around with a loser like me, anyway?'

Jill can't think of a thing to say. She has wondered the same thing herself. Finally she tries, 'Perhaps she'll come round in a week or so.'

'She's seeing someone else. It's Nigel, the captain of the rugby team. He's more in El's league. His family has pots of money. He manages a chain of motor showrooms for his father and can afford to run a swish car.'

Shaz appears in the hall doorway.

'We starting again in two minutes.' And disappears.

'Anyway, what about you and Martin? Is that still on?'

'We had lunch last week, but it's not the same. Didn't anyone tell you what happened at the party?'

For the first time Luke looks more his old self. As he and Jill make their way back into the hall he begins to chuckle.

'Martha told me about how you found old Martin on top of this chap who'd got himself done up as a woman.'

'I know everyone else thinks it funny, including Martin, but I can't get the picture of those two wrestling on the bed out of my mind. Think about it Luke. When Martin fell on top of her he didn't know that she was a him. In which case he was groping some strange woman. Or, if he did know she was a him, he was groping some strange man.'

'I expect he was just drunk.' Luke pats her arm. Jill shakes her head.

'So you're single again.'

Jill blushes. 'Well, I do see Jeremy from time to time. He's taking me out to that new club in Jute Street at the weekend.'

They resume their seats. Jill picks up her treble. 'I haven't seen much of Martha though. She seems very busy these days.'

Bridget lifts her baton and then puts it down again and gestures to Norman. 'Switch to descant for this one, Norman, as we arranged.' Norman nods and makes his way to first descants, where he shares a stand with Brenda.

Once he is settled, Bridget lifts her baton again and they begin to play the Bransles from Capriol. Bridget has set a very fast tempo. Now there is no time to think about anything else but the music.

THIRTEEN

Tuesday

Martha and her partner have been working flat out since the night of the party: a posh bash at the Inns of Court, the Operatic Society dinner, a bar mitzvah, the Feathered Friends lunch, miscellaneous engagement, birthday and one divorce party, a couple of weddings, a christening and a funeral.

Now they are on their way to a Masonic Ladies Night. They are travelling in Martha's car, which is stacked with all their gear. Most of the food for the evening is already set out in the kitchens of the Royal, the hotel where the function is to be held. Eleanor is driving while Martha goes through the order of events for the twentieth time.

'We don't start serving the first course until the master of ceremonies gives us the nod.'

'I know.'

'And there will be toasts between each course, starting with one to the . . . .'

'Ladies. Yes, I know.'

'And remember we've also got a wedding in ten days time.'

'Fine, but let me remind you that I am not working tomorrow night. Nigel is coming over to my place to cook me a meal. Isn't that sweet of him?'

'Sweet . . . but if . . . .'

'No Martha. Tomorrow night I am not working whatever happens.'

At this point, Martha's mobile phone rings. Eleanor can see from the simpering expression on her friend's face, who is calling. Although a month has elapsed since the party, Martha and George are still at the honeymoon stage of their relationship. This is partly because Martha has been so busy and partly because George had to go abroad on a business trip, which lasted over a week. Actually, to be strictly accurate, the couple is further back in their relationship than you might suppose. To put it bluntly, their relationship has not been consummated. There have been a couple of near misses, but Martha is not a back-of-the-car sort of girl so at the moment she is still technically faithful to Martin.

'George, did you get my message?' She giggles. Eleanor sighs.

'Why on earth do you want to know that?' With a stupid grin on her face – Eleanor never thought she would live to see the day – Martha says to her friend, 'He wants to know what I'm wearing.'

Eleanor negotiates a roundabout and then says sourly, 'Ask him what he is wearing.'

Martha coos into the phone: 'Eleanor wants to know what you are wearing.' She giggles again and then reports:

'He says he's sorry to disappoint you and if he had known you were going to ask, he would have put on a pink frock. As it is he's wearing a pair of aubergine slacks and a cerise shirt.'

Eleanor purses her lips but makes no comment, so Martha turns back to the phone:

'Oh all right darling, if you insist. I'm wearing my dark blue velvet skirt and that low-neck white, silk blouse and the lovely silver ear rings you brought me back from the States. Listen, we're nearly there so I'll have to ring off in a minute. No, listen. I have brilliant news. Martin is going fishing this weekend with a friend so it's on. We can go. Look, I'll meet you on Friday evening at that pub on the by-pass. We will have the whole weekend together.'

Eleanor is entering the car park of the Royal now.

'Look, I have to go darling. See you Friday.' Martha rings off.

Eleanor parks the car and then turns to look at her partner.

'So you're off for a dirty weekend with this cross dresser?'

'When I'm a white-haired old lady I will be able to boast to my grandchildren that I once had an affair with a transvestite. I expect they'll be impressed.'

'If they are Lucinda's children they will be deeply shocked. Have you told Martin?'

'No.'

'Why?'

'Because any sensible marriage is founded on a need to know basis. Martin doesn't need to know.'

Wednesday

Seven-thirty the following evening finds Eleanor dressed in a rose coloured skirt, slit to the thigh, and a crushed strawberry, low cut blouse, reclining on her white leather sofa. An Oscar Pederson Trio CD is playing quietly in the background and she is sipping champagne from a fluted glass. In her kitchen, Nigel is putting the final touches to their meal. He has already set the dining table, which is situated at the other end of the room by long sash windows overlooking the garden. From where she is sitting Eleanor can see a satisfactory array of crisp napkins, glistening silver and crystal glasses. Nigel has arranged a dozen red roses in a tall vase that he has placed in the centre of the table.

'Do you need any help?' she calls languidly.

Nigel, wearing a turquoise Timberland tee-shirt, that sets off his muscular tanned biceps to perfection and white chinos, comes into the room and announces, 'Dinner is served milady,' in a plumy voice and then moves smoothly over to one of the ladder-backed chairs beside the table and pulls it out. He bows as she moves to sit down. 'Madam.' She sits and he kisses the back of her neck.

While Eleanor unfolds her napkin, Nigel disappears into the kitchen, to return with a silver platter. On the platter are arranged a dozen or so mussels. He places the platter on the table and then sits down himself.

'For the first course, we have grilled, stuffed mussels. Shall I serve you?'

'Please,'

Carefully, Eleanor forks a mussel and some of the stuffing into her mouth. Nigel, his own fork poised, waits anxiously. Eleanor lets the man stew a little, while she takes a second and then a third mouthful. Finally she puts him out of his misery:

'Delicious. Now let's see. Chopped ham . . . .'

'Parma ham, finely minced.'

'Oregano, garlic . . . .'

'Peeled and crushed with salt and ground black pepper, of course. Anything else?'

'I don't think so.' Eleanor is getting a bit tired of all this now

'Breadcrumbs and parsley moistened with olive oil and the liquid from the mussels, which I boiled separately. Now try the wine.'

Eleanor sips and then nods. 'Perfect.'

They finish the rest of the mussels in silence, much to Eleanor's relief. Then Nigel picks up their plates and the platter of empty shells and heads back to the kitchen.

He returns carrying a large Victorian meat dish, which belonged to Eleanor's great grandmother. On the plate is a golden bird, garnished with juniper berries, mushrooms and triangles of puff pastry.

'Pheasant,' says Nigel smugly, 'with smoked bacon and mushrooms.'

Nigel places the meat dish in the centre of the table and then sets off for the kitchen once more. Eleanor can't wait to get her teeth into that succulent meat.

She looks up eagerly as Nigel returns yet again carrying a

divided dish: roast potatoes in one section and broad beans in a creamy herb sauce in the other and two plates. 'Start serving the vegetables. I'll carve the bird in a sec.' On his next return from the kitchen he brings a dish of braised red cabbage, another of glazed baby carrots and a jug of gravy. Her mouth watering, Eleanor serves out the vegetables while Nigel carves the meat.

'This is a banquet Nigel.'

Eleanor does not have to worry about putting on weight. She never puts on an ounce. She can eat like a gannet, and often does, but still keeps her sylph-like figure. Martha hates her for it. Martha puts on weight all too easily. She has only to look at a plate of chips, or so she says, and half a stone of fat gathers round her hips. The fact that Eleanor does not put on weight is, according to Martha, the severest test of the two women's friendship.

Blithely then, Eleanor helps herself to a liberal portion of the crispy pheasant, three puff pastry triangles, two rashers of the smoked bacon, red cabbage, broad beans, roast potatoes and a large splash of gravy. Without waiting to see if Nigel is ready to start eating, she sets to.

'Delicious,' she mumbles ecstatically, through a mouthful of pheasant and gravy.

'Brilliant,' stuffing red cabbage and potatoes into her mouth.

Nigel watches her with some amusement.

'I do love a woman who enjoys her food. Here, let me.'

He reaches over with a napkin and wipes a splash of gravy from her chin.

'I used porcini mushrooms . . . soaked, of course.'

'Mm.'

'And sprinkled rosemary on the puff pastry garnish.'

'Mm.'

'Then, while the puff pastry was in the oven, I spread garlic over the pheasant and seared the sides in a frying pan. Then drained it and place it in a casserole and added the juniper berries. Did you notice the juniper berries? A nice touch I thought.'

'Yes. Can you pass the gravy.'

Nigel passes the jug and then says more in sorrow than in anger, 'I made the sauce by frying the onions and bacon, stirred in the flour, the wine and the stock and then poured a good portion of it round the pheasant before I put the casserole in the oven. Finally I placed the dried and the fresh mushrooms on top. How long do you think it took to cook?' He does not wait for a reply.

'Only thirty minutes. The oven was very hot. I set it to 250. I thought of getting two pheasants because there's never that much meat on these birds but I didn't think you would have a large appetite. I made a mistake there. I can see that now.'

Eleanor looks in consternation at the meat dish. Only the carcass of the bird remains. Pity he didn't get two.

'There are some roast potatoes left though?'

'Yes please.'

'Can you eat all of them?'

There are only three potatoes left. Eleanor pauses, torn between courtesy and greed. Greed wins.

'Please.'

'Do you like the way I've cooked the broad beans?'

'Yes.' Eleanor holds out her plate and Nigel spoons the last of them onto her plate.

'I cooked them in double cream, chervil, chopped parsley, the grated zest of a lemon and minced shallots.'

Eleanor helps herself to more red cabbage, wishing that Nigel would shut up. She's really enjoying the meal but she has had quite enough of the running commentary, thank you very much.

'Shall I refill your glass?'

'Please.'

'Then I'll open another bottle.'

'Good idea.'

By the time Nigel has returned with the second bottle, Eleanor has finished everything that is on her plate and is picking the carcass, in an attempt to unearth any odd mushrooms or scraps of meat. Before he has finished pouring the wine she says,

'What's for sweet?'

Nigel has not cleared his plate yet. What with waiting on Eleanor, fetching and carrying and describing his cooking procedures, he hasn't had time. He sits down and starts to eat. After a moment he stops, looks up and finds Eleanor watching him expectantly.

'Shall I go and get the sweet?' She says.

Nigel sighs. 'The night is still young, El. I thought we might take a break before starting on the third course.

Eleanor is a bit disappointed but she is careful not to show it. She wipes her mouth with her napkin and says, 'That was truly delicious.'

Nigel smiles: 'I could see you were enjoying it.' He puts down his knife and fork.

'Actually, I've had enough. Do you want to finish . . .?'

'Pass it over.'

The rugby captain watches in astonishment as this fragile-looking woman rapidly demolishes all that is left on his plate.

When she has finished, Eleanor gets up. 'I'll clear.' As Nigel begins to protest, 'No, I mean it. Go and listen to the Oscar Pederson.'

Nigel protests no further. Suddenly, he feels quite exhausted. Not surprising considering all the cutting, slicing and scraping, the boiling and roasting, the polishing and setting he has done today. He moves to the sofa and lies down, while Eleanor begins

135

to stack the plates and containers and clear the table.

Finally she carries the first consignment of dishes into the kitchen, where she looks round in dismay. The ceramic hob is glistening with grease and something has burnt into the front ring. There are vegetable peelings and mussel shells in the sink. Every surface is covered with mixing bowls, pans, the pastry board, plastic containers, kitchen utensils. As far as she can see Nigel has used every single pan, container, bowl, casserole, kitchen utensil that she owns. Grimly, she stacks, scrapes, empties, puts into soak (two burnt pans that she's not sure that she can salvage at this point) and finally begins to fill the dish-washer. She can hear Nigel whistling to the Oscar Pederson CD. She half expects him to come to her assistance, but it is clear that Nigel thinks he has done his share for the evening thank you very much. When she cannot fit another teaspoon into the dishwasher, she turns it on and then cleans out the sink and puts her grandmother's meat dish in soak. Finally she cleans the hob and swabs down all the work surfaces. She decides to leave the floor until the morning.

After all that exertion Eleanor feels that she has earned her pudding. Anyway, she's still feeling a bit peckish. She looks inside the refrigerator and finds a lemon soufflé, a cheesecake and a jug of cream. She also locates a selection of cheeses. She takes down dishes and desert plates from her kitchen cupboards and carries them, together with the cheeses into the dining area.

Nigel is lying full length on the sofa. He holds out his arms. It's pretty clear what he wants for 'sweet'. After all that cleaning and scraping that's the last thing Eleanor has in mind. Ignoring Nigel she sets the table with dishes, plates and cutlery. Then she fetches the soufflé, cheesecake and jug of cream and places them also on the table.

Undeterred Nigel pats the sofa and says, 'Come and sit down darling. I thought we'd eat the sweets later.'

Eleanor seats herself at the table and cuts herself a large slice of cheesecake. She pours a generous helping of cream onto the cheesecake.

'This is later.' She looks at her watch. 'Nearly thirty minutes later. It's taken me all that time to sort out the mess you left in my kitchen.'

Reluctantly, Nigel drags himself to his feet. He sits down at the table but makes no move to eat. Instead he watches his new girl friend munch her way through a large piece of his cheesecake.

Eleanor finishes her cheesecake and then pauses for a moment. She really enjoyed the cheesecake and she is toying with the idea of helping herself to another slice. On the other hand she is a bit full now and she would like some soufflé. She helps herself to the soufflé. This worries Nigel a little.'

'Didn't you like the cheesecake?'

'It was lovely but. . . .'

'Well I'll tell you how I made it. I used ricotta . . . .'

But Eleanor has had enough. 'Don't tell me Nigel. I really don't want to know. I don't want to know how you made the cheesecake or where you bought the cheese and I don't want to know how many eggs you used for the soufflé either.'

'As a matter of fact I . . . .'

'Nigel!' she says, warningly.

'It's just that there's this marvellous delicatessen in . . . .'

'I am not interested Nigel.'

'I thought that, since you are a professional cook, you would be.' Nigel is a little hurt.

'When I cook, I cook. When I eat, I eat. And when I eat I don't want to know how what I am eating was cooked, or even from where it was bought, I just want to enjoy eating it.'

Nigel still isn't satisfied. He says anxiously, 'But you have enjoyed my cooking.'

'For Christ's sake, Nigel! Of course I have. You can see

that I have. Did I pick at my food? No I didn't. What do you want? A round of applause?'

Nigel grins. He has a nice smile and lots of very white teeth and there's no doubt about it, the man can cook. Eleanor reaches out and takes one of his large brown hands. 'It was a fantastic meal and I didn't cook it. Sometimes I feel cooked out.'

'You don't know how pleased I am to hear that.'

Nigel stands. 'Go and sit down. I'll make the coffee and I have a good Cognac to go with it.'

After the coffee and brandy, Eleanor lies back in the crook of her boyfriend's arm and wonders if either of them have the energy to finish off the evening as it deserves. She looks up at Nigel through her eyelashes and sees that his eyes are closed. He's not asleep though because one hand is gently caressing her arm, sending little shivers through her entire body. She and Nigel have made love a couple of times now, once at his flat and once here on this very couch. He's a definite seven out of ten, and might with a bit of encouragement rise to the dizzy heights of nine. Not tonight though. Neither of them is up to it tonight. No, the truth is she's too tired, she decides.

Nigel kisses the top of her head and to her alarm, says, 'I have a proposal I want to put to you El.' Is he about to propose? Eleanor hopes not. It's much too soon. Luke proposed and look what happened then.

'More of a proposition really.'

'What kind of proposition?' Eleanor pulls herself into a sitting position and turns so that she can see Nigel's face more clearly.

'A business proposition.'

Eleanor places both feet on the floor. This is not at all what she was expecting. She tries to gather her thoughts. This is not easy after champagne, wine and brandy, not to mention a large meal.

Nigel shifts along the couch, putting some distance between himself and Eleanor.

'You know that I work in partnership with my father in the family business?'

Eleanor shrugs. 'I suppose. I've never really thought much about how you earn your living.'

'I manage a number of motor outlets as a matter of fact and up until recently our company has been only concerned with the selling and maintenance of Fiats. We have the franchise for this area. My father's an entrepreneur. He started with one small garage, when he was in his early twenties and now he owns a chain. Now he's diversifying. Last year he bought a run down antique shop in Hertford. Recently, he bought new premises – Hammonds in the High Street.'

Eleanor looks up with interest. 'I remember Hammonds. I bought a really smart frock there about five years ago. What's your father going to do with the premises?'

'My father has left the decision up to me.'

'And what are you going to do with it?'

'Well I'd like to reopen it as a boutique. I envisage a really trendy, bang up to date store, a place to which every fashion conscious woman might make a beeline at least once a week. But what I need to find is the right manager, someone with flare, someone with an eye for colour and design. Someone just like you, darling.'

Eleanor tries to clear her head. 'I already have a job,' she says.

'I know but I'm offering you another one. You would be ideal. You could have a completely free hand. The shop that was has been gutted. You could design the interior of the new one. I've only to look round this room to know that you have an eye for interior design.

Eleanor is immediately tempted by the idea but she does

have doubts.

'I'm not sure that I'd know where to start, when it came to stocking the shop and I assume that you would want me to do all the buying, choose the clothes myself.'

Nigel nods, delighted that Eleanor is interested in his proposition.

'I used to know where to locate the outlets of the big labels, but I've been out of the business for so long.'

'We'd give you time to find your feet. Of course you would have to do masses of research but within a time frame of say a year, I'm confident you would get up to speed.'

Eleanor gets up. 'I think I'll make some more coffee.'

Nigel follows her into the kitchen and continues his sales pitch while she grinds coffee beans, fills the kettle and takes down clean mugs.

'I have a friend, who is the buyer for a chain of boutiques in London. We were at art college together,' she says.

'You went to art college? I didn't know that.'

'I didn't finish the course. I took up modelling instead.'

'Eleanor, you know you are interested. Just give me a perhaps.'

'Yes, no. I don't know. Anyway, what about Martha?'

'What about her?'

'We're partners. After I stopped modelling, I had a disastrous long-term affair with a professional photographer and a series of dead end jobs. Martha rescued me from the affair and the pointless jobs. We set up the business together.'

'But it's called Martha's Kitchen.'

'Because the whole idea was hers. We've both been in it together from the beginning though.'

'How long?'

'Well, if you count the first year, when we only got one

booking every month, ten years.. We've even talked of opening a restaurant.'

'Funny you should say that. My father's just bought a property in Little Melding that was a restaurant for a time.'

'Little Melding? I know the restaurant you mean. It was called the Blue Hyacinth but it's been closed for some years now.'

'Perhaps Martha should look at the premises.'

'She hasn't got that kind of money, neither has Martin.'

'We're moving away from the main subject: the boutique. What do you say?'

Eleanor pours water into the cafeteria.

'I'll think about it.'

FOURTEEN

Still Wednesday

The same evening that Nigel prepares his cordon bleu meal for Eleanor, the Breman family is dining at home. Martin, who has just placed a platter of sausages and chops with the mash, on the table, calls from the dining room, 'Come and eat.'

Martin waits for everyone to be seated. 'Well. Isn't this nice. Just like old times.'

Martha looks sourly from one member of her family to another. 'Lovely,' she says. Martin ignores her.

'You all seem to lead such hectic lives these days. Last night I ate on my own and the night before that and the night before that it was just me and Jeremy and . . . .'

'All right, Martin, we don't want a blow by blow account. The reason why I haven't sat down to a meal with my family lately is because I've been working.'

'Where were you working Sunday night?'says Lucinda innocently.

Martha has no intention of discussing what she was doing on Sunday evening right now, so she changes the subject briskly, 'I really need another freezer, Martin.'

'We already have three freezers, four, if you count the drawers below the fridge. You are not getting another one.'

'Then how am I to manage?'

'Don't take on so much work. It's all getting out of hand, Martha. I hope you are not working this weekend.'

'It won't affect you, whatever I do this weekend. You're going fishing with Jake.'

'No, I'm not. He rang me up to say he couldn't make it. Perhaps you and I . . . .'

'But you must go fishing. It's all arranged. You've been

looking forward to it.'

'It's not that im . . . .'

'And you've ordered the bait.'

'No. I just rang the shop to make sure they'd have some in on Saturday.'

'And booked a room at the King's Arms.'

'I can unbook it.'

'Jeremy, why don't you go fishing with your father?'

'I don't fish.'

'You used to fish . . . with your father.'

'When I was ten.'

Lucinda looks at her younger brother with disdain. 'Don't expect Jeremy to come fishing with you, dad. He'd have to get out of bed early. Anyway fishing is too energetic for little brother. I mean you have to move your arms.'

Stung, Jeremy says, 'Yeah, dad. You're on. Tomorrow I'll get a rod out and practise my casting.'

'We might as well drive down on Friday night.'

Martha smiles benevolently on her son and husband. 'Well, that's settled then,' she says.

Thursday

Jill and Jeremy are sitting in the garden of a pub on the outskirts of town enjoying an unseasonably warm evening. Jill, wearing pale green trousers with matching crop top, is staring moodily at Jeremy who is leafing through a fishing magazine.

'What I really need is a heavy duty rod. My old Nimrod is too light for sea fishing.'

'So you are determined to go fishing this weekend?'

'Yeah . . . like I said . . . .'

'But you promised to take me to the new club in Jute Street on Saturday night.'

'Well we can go out clubbing next week. How about

Monday night?'

'I play recorder on Monday nights.'

'Can't you give it a miss for once?'

'No. We've got a concert coming up.'

Suddenly the young woman realises that she is wasting her time with Jeremy. It's time to move on. She is just about to make her excuses and leave, when she spots a heavily built man enter the saloon door of the pub.

'Jeremy,' she says. 'Isn't that Manfred going into the bar?'

Jeremy looks up, but the man has disappeared inside. He shrugs.

'He was on his own and he looked, I don't know, sort of lonely, sort of bereft.'

'You could tell all that just by watching him go through a door?'

'He's bound to be feeling down, isn't he? Your sister's dumped him again hasn't she? Go and see if it is him.'

'And what am I supposed to say?'

Jill gets to her feet. 'Well if you won't, I will. I'm going to suggest that he joins us. Have you got a problem with that?'

Before Jeremy can think of a suitably crushing reply, Jill has disappeared into the pub. She enters the saloon bar: red plastic tables and imitation leather chairs, brass topped bar, chandeliers, glittering juke box and barmaid proudly displaying her new implants, and looks around for Manfred. Most of the chairs are occupied but there is only one man sitting on a high stool by the bar. It is the horn player and he is gazing despondently into a glass of lager. Jill walks straight up to him and says brightly, 'Hallo Manfred. I hope you don't mind me accosting you like this but we, that's Jeremy and me, were wondering if you would like to come over and join us.'

Manfred looks up from his drink in surprise. 'You can accost me any day of the week you like er . . . .'

'I'm Jill, Jill Peters. We've sort of met a couple of times, the last was at Eleanor's party.'

His face clears. 'The party where I passed out on the patio?'

Jill grins. 'That's the one. I thought you looked very peaceful lying among the geraniums. Jeremy and I are sitting outside. Do join us.'

Manfred needs no persuasion. He follows Jill out into the garden where he spots Jeremy sitting with another bloke under a tree. Luke has joined him.

'What are you all having to drink?' says Luke.

Jeremy and Luke disappear into the pub to get the drinks so Jill settles herself down beside Manfred and begins to gush, 'I've been dying to meet you. Properly I mean. Martha told me that you were a professional musician, a French Horn player. I absolutely adore the French Horn.'

She pauses for breath but before Manfred can say a word, plunges on: 'I adore music. I always have, ever since I was a very small child. I think I like Mozart best. But there again, when I'm listening to say Ravel, I'm not so sure.' Another quick gulp of air and she's off again:

'I would never be good enough to be a professional, but I do feel that deep down in my soul I, too, am a musician. I'm a pianist.'

'That's nice,' he says noncommittally. Jill is still looking at him expectantly, so he adds lamely, 'What kind of things do you play?'

'Well, I haven't had a lot of chance to practise lately because we've been so busy, but I was working on a couple of the Chopin Etudes, the A flat Opus 10 Number one and the C minor. I did the A flat for my Grade 8.'

Manfred looks at Jill with renewed respect.

'My teacher wanted me to try for music college, but I knew I wasn't good enough.'

Before Manfred can think of a reply, Luke and Jeremy return with the drinks.

Taking her wine from Jeremy, Jill says, 'Manfred and I have been talking about music.'

Luke sits down opposite Manfred and says, 'I went to a marvellous performance of Britten's Serenade for horn, tenor and strings last year at the Festival Hall.'

'I've played it,' says Manfred. 'Let's see, the performance was at Guild Hall in Cambridge about eighteen months ago. Robert Bernard sang the tenor part.' Jill gazes at Manfred with wide admiring eyes. She is actually sitting next to a man who has performed the solo horn in the Britten Serenade. And he's just sitting there, sipping his beer like any ordinary mortal. There's something noble about his humility, she thinks.

'I'd so love to hear you play,' she whispers. Jeremy looks glumly into his beer. He picks up his fishing magazine.

'I'm playing the solo horn in the Shostakovich first cello concerto in Bournemouth next weekend. I can get you a ticket if you like.'

'Could you Manfred? I would love that.'

'If you don't mind travelling down early, we've got a rehearsal in the afternoon, I can give you a lift. We could get there in time for lunch. If you wanted to, you could sit in on the rehearsal.'

'Oh Manfred, could I?'

'Sure, why not?'

'I've got a marvellous recording of the first cello concerto,' says Luke eagerly. 'Rostropovich is playing.'

Jeremy turns to the advertisement section of his magazine. Might as well price a few rods.

FIFTEEN

Friday

Martha drives into the car park of the Black Swan early Friday evening, still half wondering whether it might not be wiser to turn the car right round and return home. Going away for the weekend with George seemed such a good idea at the time: so romantic, so liberating, so . . . show Martin she too could have an affair. Now she is having cold feet.

Martin and Jeremy had spent the day preparing for their fishing trip. Judging by the pile of gear they had amassed, they might as well have been planning an assault on Everest. When she went upstairs to pack herself, she found her husband trying to close a large suitcase.

He looked up irritably: 'Have you seen my thick, navy socks?'

'No, Martin.'

Muttering to himself he went out on the landing and shouted down to Jeremy who was moving the gear from the hall into his father's car:

'Check that we've got enough floats Jeremy and my rod carrier's in the dining room.'

Martha took down a small pig skin travelling case from the top shelf of the fitted cupboards and put into it a night dress, her blue velvet skirt, a matching top, her favourite roll neck sweater, a pair of jeans, a striped tee shirt, a fleece and toilet bag. Then she removed her new cherry-red suit and cream chiffon blouse from their protective covers and put them on together with a pair of black high-heeled boots. Finally, she applied make-up and sprayed herself lavishly with an expensive French perfume. Martin returned to the bedroom as Martha finished her toilette. He heaved his now closed case off the bed and dragged it with some difficulty out on the landing.

'Leave room in the boot for my case Jeremy and have you kept out a flask for the journey?' he called as he clattered downstairs.

Martha checked her case, closed it and then went to the bedroom window and looked down at the drive, where she could see her son and husband loading Martin's case and a crate of beer into the already over-crowded back seat of Martin's Volvo.

She walked slowly down the stairs and met her husband in the hall by the front door. At last he noticed the case.

'Where are you off to?' Before she could reply he shouted through the open door, 'Jeremy, you did remember to order the bait didn't you?'

'Yes, dad.'

'Excuse me,' said Martha as she walked past her husband, 'I'm off now.'

Something must have registered with Martin then because he came after her and said, 'Where did you say you were going?'

Martha paused on the drive, her car was parked on the road, and looked back at her husband, who was peering anxiously up at his rods, perched precariously on the roof rack.

'I'm going away for the weekend with a friend.'

'Jeremy, you'll have to secure those rods better than that.'

Martha climbed into her car and drove away.

Martha watches George expertly swing his BMW into the car park of the Black Swan. It is too late to back out now, she reflects. When they meet, he takes her in his arms, kisses her and then holds her back so that he can get a better a view.

'You look absolutely stunning,' he says and then kisses her again. 'Red is definitely your colour.'

Martha smiles. This is more like it.

A minute later she is sitting in George's car and they are

roaring off down the by-pass. Without taking his eyes off the road, George lifts her hand and carries it to his lips.

'Where are we going?' She asks.

'I've booked us into a lovely little pub in Orford. There's an excellent restaurant attached and I've reserved a room with a large four poster bed.'

The journey to Orford takes over two hours so it is getting on for eight when George and Martha check into the Falcon. Light pours out from the latticed windows and although it is dark now, Martha can just make out weathered red brick, a steeply pitched roof with dormer windows and a studded door that swings open to admit them. They enter a low ceiling room with dark beams, gleaming brasses, a roaring fire and capacious button-back chairs. A smiling middle-aged woman emerges from behind a dark oak desk to greet them.

George says easily, 'Perhaps you can arrange for someone to take up our bags – just the two.' Pointing to Martha's pigskin and his black leather cases. 'We'll sit here in the bar for a few minutes and I suggest that you bring us a couple of drinks: a gin and tonic and a vodka and tonic. I ordered the lobster if you remember. We'll eat in say twenty minutes.'

And that sets the tone for the entire weekend. George takes charge, makes all the decisions without consultation and Martha finds herself going along with whatever he decides. She finds all this very restful at first. By Sunday the novelty has worn off. By then, Martha is more than a little tired of playing the squaw.

Not the first night though. That first night she allows herself to be told what to eat and what to drink. She does not argue when, after a delicious lobster thermidor with a crisp Pinot Grigio to accompany it, George waves away the trolley of delicious looking sweets and orders a ripe Brie instead. She gazes adoringly (like a US president's wife) at her soon-to-be-lover while he entertains her with a stream of anecdotes, mainly centred round his various travel adventures.

Martha is vastly entertained, but she is also very tired. George is talking about a trip he made to Japan now, but Martha is no longer listening. She is reflecting on the fact that this attractive man, with whom she's about to go to bed, is a virtual stranger. She's only known him a month when all's said and done and during that month has been in his company four, no, five times, if you count the party. They met for a meal in a swish restaurant last Sunday and the weekend after Eleanor's engagement party he had taken her to a play at the National. Now a whole weekend looms ahead — two days and two nights. George suddenly tunes into the fact that he no longer has Martha's undivided attention. He stands, takes the half empty brandy glass from her hand and places it on the table.

'Come on,' he says masterfully. 'Time to go, I think.'

George and Martha make their way up a winding staircase to their room, which is on the first floor. The room is small but snug and welcoming. The light from two pink shaded lamps placed either side of the large four poster bed casts a warm glow over a white lacy coverlet, frilly white curtains and deep shadows on the low ceiling. There is also a walnut wardrobe, a basket chair with pretty patchwork cushions and a dressing table on which is placed a bowl of purple and mauve chrysanthemums. To one side of the wardrobe is a low doorway, which leads into a pink and white tiled bath room and shower unit

Martha, not at all sure how to play this scene, takes a couple of hesitant steps into the room. Should she unpack? Undress? Perhaps she should throw herself impetuously onto the bed and hold out her arms.

Needless to say, George knows exactly what to do. He

grasps her masterfully in his arms then begins to kiss her comprehensively. First on the lips – deep and long – and then fluttering kisses on each closed eye, along her cheeks, round and inside her ears and then, after slipping off her jacket, he starts on her neck. Next George removes her blouse and unzips her skirt. Within seconds it is round her ankles and she is standing in her new silk slip, briefs, bra, tights and high-heeled boots. Feeling rather chilly and very self conscious, she sits down on the edge of the bed and leans forward to remove her boots but George kneels down and stops her.

'No,' he says commandingly. 'I will do everything. Stand up again.' She stands and allows him to unzip her boots. She steps out of them. Now he reaches beneath the skirt of her slip and removes first her briefs and then her tights. As his hands slide over her thighs and once – deliberately – between her legs, she feels the first shiver of desire.

Finally, he lifts her slip over her head and unhooks her bra. Martha is standing stark naked and George is still fully clothed. She is not entirely happy about this but now, still making no effort to remove his clothes, George gently presses her back onto the bed and arranges her with her head resting against one of the pillows. Lifting her hips, he places the other – and this entails a lot of wriggling, heaving and manoeuvring on Martha's part – beneath her hips. She has no idea why he does this and doesn't like to ask. Then he lies down beside her. 'Do you like it when I touch your breasts?'

Martha does not reply but she is thoroughly roused. Never-theless, there is one small part of her mind just looking on and that part of her is exercised because George is still fully clothed. He hasn't even taken his shoes off for god's sake. She reaches for his zip, but the man will have none of it. He stays her hand.

'Is this what you like?' He says. She does not reply, partly because she is incapable of speech. 'Tell me what you want me to do.' He continues. 'Do you like it when I touch you like this and this?'

Martha is panting now and she knows that if he doesn't stop soon she will come. Even so, the separate part, even now, is exasperated with George. Of course she is enjoying what he is doing but she has no desire to explain or talk about it. He is still murmuring away about how silky she feels inside and is he doing what she wants. He must see what she wants. Does he want her to spell it out? Why is he playing games? It is perfectly obvious what she wants and if he doesn't stop messing about, she will come before he's taken his trousers off.

Perhaps George realises this himself, because he suddenly pulls away from her, stands and then begins to undress swiftly and efficiently. He has an erection, Martha notes through half closed eyes, but it isn't huge. Momentarily, she compares him with Martin, but then pushes the thought away as George positions himself on top of her and with no further preliminaries, thrusts inside. Within seconds Martha comes and with no sound.

Although George must feel the tension slide from her body, he continues for some time. Then he slumps for what seems forever between her legs. Martha loses all sensation in her right arm and then her left leg. She is uncomfortable and bored. If it was Martin, she would have told him to move ages ago, but this isn't Martin so she waits with increasing discomfort, until, at last, George heaves himself away, arranges himself at her side and draws her head onto his chest.

All Martha wants to do is to wash, curl up and then go to sleep. But unfortunately George has other plans.

He kisses the top of her head and says with a complacent smile in his voice, 'Now tell me, how was it for you?'

'Lovely, thank you,' says Martha in a small voice, feeling both irritated and silly at the same time.

George turns to examine her face. 'Really?' She can see that her response is less than expected. She nearly asks him if he wants her to award stars or a marks out of ten, but decides, probably wisely, against it. Instead she says, trying to instil more enthusiasm into her voice 'Really. I had a simply wonderful time.' And it's true. She has enjoyed herself but now she wants to sleep.

'Well I thought so, but I just wanted to be quite sure. You're more inhibited, Martha, than I expected. I expected you to, well, make it clear what you wanted. I could have gone on longer if you'd wanted.'

'I liked it just how it was.'

'Don't hold back from me, Martha. '

Martha is too tired to argue. She likes sex – she always has – but she is not a great one for talking about it. She has never thought of sex as a talking activity, more a just getting on and doing it sort of activity. And once it's over she likes to sleep and naturally is dismayed when she realises George has other plans.

He idly begins to caress her right breast again and she really does not want him to do that right now. He settles himself more comfortably against the pillows and says, 'The truth is that everyone is different. Everyone has different needs. You are a deeply sensuous and sexy lady, but I don't think you have ever really explored your sexuality. You and I are going to explore that sexuality together this weekend. The position, the angle, can make all the difference to the pleasure. You must say which position is best for you.'

Martha and Martin are not the most adventurous of lovers. They have tried three, possibly four positions at the most. Martha knows there are many others, but she has no idea what they are. She's not even sure she wants to find out. George is still rambling on but she's not listening.

George has no idea that he is almost the first man Martha has slept with since she married Martin. He believes that Martha has a very liberal and modern attitude to sex. He assumes that she has had a number of affairs.

'George, I . . . .'

'Trust me.'

He rolls her over, slides her down the bed, until she is kneeling over the end and attempts to mount her from behind. Martha is not happy.

'I loved what you did, George, I really did, but I won't come again, I know it. '

She is wasting her breath, so she lies still and lets him beaver away. He manoeuvres her into various undignified positions all to no avail. Whatever erogenous zones he's after, he doesn't find them. At last, to Martha's infinite relief, he gives up, rolls back onto the bed and is soon snoring. She has a quick shower, finds her nightdress, puts it on and then with a sigh sinks into bed beside George.

For a few minutes she ponders about all that has happened since she and George came upstairs. Part of her can't help wondering though if he's working his way through some manual or other.

Martha, by today's standards, is a virgin. She only went the whole way – as she puts it - with two of her boyfriends before she started going out with Martin. And she did not climax with either. The third time she and Martin had sex, she reached orgasm. Within a year of meeting, they were married, although Martin was still in his final year at university.

Martha has been faithful to Martin by and large. She doesn't count the brief sordid quickie after a party with a lecherous neighbour. She hardly felt a thing, she was so anaesthetised by drink. Neither does she count the long languorous kiss on the way home from a PTA meeting with one of the other parents.

There had been other opportunities apart from the two mentioned, for Martha is an attractive woman with the kind of breasts men admire, but each time an opportunity arose for her to experiment outside her marriage, she found herself too exhausted to do anything about it. Bringing up two children, looking after an ailing mother, which she did for a time during her late thirties, and doing a full time job for most of her married life, left her little energy for extra-marital affairs.

And that is why Martha has no idea if George's obsessive activities in bed are the usual thing or not. As she falls asleep, her last conscious thought is: 'I've trod the straight and narrow up until tonight, but I'm making up for lost time now.'

SIXTEEN

Saturday

Martha is awakened by a kiss on the forehead. Reluctantly, she opens her eyes and then closes them again quickly. For a moment her mind beats around the inside of her brain in total panic. Who is the dark figure looming over her? Where is she? Who is she?

Then it all comes flooding back. Slowly she pulls herself into a sitting position. George draws the curtains and bright sunlight pours like liquid gold into the room. Martha is uninterested in the golden sunlight. She is sluggish and bad-tempered in the morning. Reluctantly she opens her eyes again and peers up at George, who she can now see is holding a cup and saucer in his right hand. He is fully dressed and wearing maroon cords, a navy blue polo sweater under a burgundy-coloured anorak. Round his neck is slung a pair of binoculars. Clearly George is a morning person and irritatingly bright-eyed and bushy-tailed. She takes the cup and sips. It is coffee.

'I don't like. . . .' then thinks better of it. This isn't Martin, after all, and drinks the hot liquid, which is strong and unsweetened – just how she doesn't like it.

'Feeling better?'

No. 'What time is it?'

'Nine fifteen. Shall I order your breakfast to be brought up?'

'Have you eaten?'

'Ages ago.' He picks up the phone.

'Can you bring up a pot of coffee, toast, fruit juice to number five? Thank you.'

'I might have wanted bacon and egg.'

'Well you are having toast and marmalade. It will be up in

a minute. I suggest you shower before you eat.'

'What time did you get up?' Where is the obsessive lover of the night before?

'Seven. I just had a coffee and then I went down to the quay and along the river.'

'You went for a walk at seven o'clock in the morning? What ever for?'

'It was a bit late but I saw an avocet, oyster catchers and widgeon of course and . . . .'

'I had no idea you were interested in birds.'

' I also saw reed buntings, a red shank and I thought I saw a godwit, but it's a bit early for winter visitors so I might have been mistaken.'

Did he say godwit?

'It's a lovely day. The sky is blue and the sun's shining. We're going to Aldeburgh this morning. We could walk along the coast,'

Martha does not do walking. She is the kind of woman who will circle round and round looking for a parking space, rather than park on the edge of town and walk in. Perhaps George senses this for he continues: 'But it's over four miles and I'm not sure where to cross the river. No, we'll go by car. The wetlands round Aldeburgh are marvellous for wild life. I've spotted bitterns and harriers there before now.'

Martha just can't keep up and that's the truth. Especially at nine twenty in the morning after an energetic night before. This man is constantly surprising her and she is finding it very unsettling. First she had filed him under: 'Duncan's dad' – charming, dashing but still simply the father of her son's best friend. Then he metamorphosed into transvestite Duncan's dad, which was exciting but also a little disappointing, since at that point she assumed he was gay. But this turned out to be wrong. How could he be gay when he made love to her so relentlessly the night before?

The man's too clever by half. He's so well read that he makes Martha, who has read obsessively since she was ten, feel illiterate. On top of that he has travelled to India, Borneo, South America and she wouldn't be at all surprised to discover that he's climbed Everest. Now it turns out that he's a bird-watcher as well. Perhaps he trains lions. Perhaps he can play the flugal horn. He could be one of the great train robbers as far as she knows. He might be a personal friend of Osama Ben Laden.

There is a knock on the bedroom door. It is a waitress with Martha's breakfast. George takes the tray and places it on the bedside table. He moves to the door and says, 'You finish your breakfast. I'll meet you downstairs at ten.' And he is gone.

Dressed in jeans, blue and white striped tee shirt and carrying her navy fleece over one arm, Martha is in the reception area of the bar promptly at ten. This is just as well because George is pacing up and down by the door. He guides her through it saying, 'We'll walk down to the quay, give you a chance to stretch your legs, and then I think you should see Orford castle and I want to book a table for tonight at the Oyster restaurant. After that we'll drive to Aldeburgh, where we'll have lunch. There's one of the best fish and chips shops in the entire country there.'

They stroll down a long sloping street of terracotta-coloured terraced cottages, with a grey, square Norman church at one end, until they reach the river and a square stone jetty that looks out over the water.

'I moored a sailing dinghy here for some time and sailed down the east coast as far as Inverness one year.'

So he's a sailor as well as a twitcher and a transvestite. Is there no end to the man's talents?

Later they drive into Aldeburgh and Martha is immediately charmed. George and Martha wander along the High Street admiring the pink, yellow and blue-washed houses and shops, the terraced cottages, the Georgian facades. There is no shopping precinct, no Tescos or Sainsburys, no Top Shop or Next.

'It's like going back in time,' says George. As usual he is right.

The beach and the adjacent 'front' runs parallel to the High Street. It's out of season now and the rows of hotels and boarding houses with their red, gabled roofs look deserted.

George buys the fish and chips and he and Martha find a bench near the life-boat station and tuck in. She glances sideways at George. He looks good, dark hair ruffled by the stiff breeze, face glowing. His eyes are following a flight of gulls as they loop and soar above the waves. He turns and meets her gaze.

'Now this afternoon we are going to Snape. I want to show you the Maltings, the concert hall that Benjamin Britten and Peter Pears founded.

Martha likes Snape. They wander down to the river first. George gets out his binoculars and looks across the reeds.

'There's a reed warbler over there. Martha looks but can see nothing but waving reeds.

'You can follow a path through these marshes and reed beds for quite a way but we can do that another time.' Another time?

'These salt marshes are really special if you are into nature. Today though, I'll let you explore the shops.'

Martha enjoys the shops. Then they wander round a gallery, where an exhibition of paintings by local artists is on display. Martha is particularly taken by an impressionistic water colour painting of the reed beds. Finally they skirt the concert hall and George stops to pick up a pamphlet detailing forthcoming events at a kiosk by the box office. Through one of the windows along the side of the building, Martha spots a young Chinese girl practising a cello.

'Have you been to any concerts at the Maltings?'

'Yes,' says George. Wouldn't you know it.

'I saw a production of Peter Grimes here some time ago and last year I came to a couple of chamber music concerts.'

They sit down on a bench overlooking the reed beds and George stretches his arm along behind Martha's shoulders. He kisses her lightly on her cheek and says, 'I want to know how your campaign to get Jill and Martin together is progressing.'

Martha laughs. 'It isn't progressing at all. You finally gave the kiss of death to their relationship, when you tried to seduce my husband.'

'He was definitely smitten. I make a dashed attractive woman, if I say it as shouldn't. If that young woman hadn't burst into the bedroom when she did, who knows what might have happened.'

'Unfortunately, Jill seems more interested in my son than in my husband these days.'

George laughs and then rises to his feet. 'Let's go back to the hotel.'

'OK, but why the sudden rush?'

I want to make love to you again.'

The love-making follows a similar pattern to the night before, but Martha is more prepared this time and less tired. Again George is tireless in his efforts to please but what he doesn't seem able to understand is that Martha is not the multi-orgasm sexual acrobat that he seems to imagine she is. She comes quickly again, but then loses interest in the entire proceedings. Martha endures it though without protest. It seems only polite seeing as George is making such strenuous efforts.

They dine later that evening in the Oyster Bar, rather Spartan in décor, well no décor at all really, just bare scrubbed tables and red plastic chairs, but the food is superb and so is the wine. They have grilled oysters followed by baked sea bass. When they return to the hotel, which is just across the square, at about eleven, they go straight up to their room and to Martha's relief, George undresses and is soon sleep.

Sunday.
Next morning, George wakes Martha at six. Not for sex. When she finds out what he has in mind, Martha thinks sex would be preferable.

'Come on Martha. Get up. I'm taking you bird-watching.' George is already dressed – roll neck sweater, jeans and studded walking boots. He has a cup of coffee in his hand, which after a sulky pause, Martha takes.

At six twenty she is slumped bleary-eyed beside her lover in his BMW looking bad-temperedly at the birch and Scotch pines of the Tunstall forest. They slip through silent Suffolk villages but the pastel coloured houses have lost their charm, and, finally, arrive at a junction, where George rolls the car to a halt. Martha can see a signpost at the fork in the road. One arm of the signpost points straight on to Dunwich and the other to the Mimsmere Bird Sanctuary. George swings into a narrow lane, barely the width of the car, with trees just beginning to turn into their golden autumn leaf, arching overhead.

Martha looks back to the fork. 'George, that other sign says Dunwich.'

'Yes. We are only a couple of miles from Dunwich beach,' agrees George as he carefully negotiates the pot holes in the twisting lane.

'Martin and Jeremy are fishing on Dunwich beach. They might be there now.'

'Shall we go along and say hello, I'm game if you are.'

She knows he is bluffing but is not absolutely certain. What if she agrees and he sets off for Dunwich? George looks at her questioningly. 'Your choice.'

'Let's go bird watching.' Martha can't believe she said that. George parks the BMW in the car park of the visitors' centre and leads Martha to the beach.

Exposed to a brisk easterly wind, they are soon standing on steeply shelving shingle looking out onto the north sea, which glitters in the bright morning sun like a huge bronze shield. George points out three oyster catches, skimming the tops of the waves and a flight of geese heading inland.

Martha spends the next four hours walking the nature trails of the Minsmere bird sanctuary. She follows George along pathways that meander through woodland and heathland and finally down to a small lake. There they watch the arrival, or so George tells her, of winter visitors. She squelches, moaning softly to herself, through reed beds and mud banks and sits in wooden hides gazing out on marsh or waterway waiting for the elusive otter that George assures her will appear, but never does. By eleven o'clock, she is so tired that she is sure that she cannot walk another step. She is also very hungry. They are following a trail with gorse bushes on either side, through open heathland now.

'I saw a bittern here last Spring,' George whispers. He has not spoken above a low murmur all morning. Who does he think he is? David Attenborough?

'We're only about three miles from the car, now. We should be back at Orford in time for lunch.'

Three miles! As they set off once again, Martha vows that once she gets back to the hotel, she will refuse to walk another step. Nature's all very well, but enough is enough. Her legs ache and so does her back and there's a blister on her left heel, which means her foot will have to be amputated.

When they finally get back to the hotel, George takes Martha up to their room and runs her a hot bath. When she emerges from the bath half an hour later, she finds that he has persuaded the restaurant to send a meal up to their room. Wrapped in a large white towel, Martha gulps down French Onion Soup, consumes the Chicken Chasseur and drinks more than her fair share of a bottle of white wine, and then allows herself to be coaxed back to bed. By George's standards, the love making is perfunctory (forty minutes including extensive fore-play) and when it's all over, Martha sinks into an exhausted sleep.

The illicit weekend is all over bar the shouting. Early evening finds the couple, packed, bill paid, by George of course, climbing into his BMW for the journey home. They stop for a couple of hours on the way back at an expensive restaurant. It is gone eleven, therefore, before they drive at the car park of the Black Swan, where Martha has left her vehicle.

She does not know it, but Martin and Jeremy have been home from their fishing trip for three hours. During those three hours Martin has whined plaintively fourteen times, Jeremy has kept count, 'I can't think where your mother is. Are you sure she didn't say where she was going?'

SEVENTEEN

October. Friday morning 10 a.m.

Martha Breman is fed up. All the preparations for tomorrow night's gig – a party to be held after the long awaited recorder orchestra concert – has fallen on Martha's shoulders. Eleanor, notionally still a fully paid-up partner, seems to have lost interest in "Martha's Kitchen".' She spends a good proportion of her time at the shop. All she can talk about these days is: curtains, carpeting, wall lighting, changing rooms, designer labels. Martha has tried various stratagems to make her friend change her mind including bullying. 'Eleanor, you are not to take this job. Have I made myself clear?'

She's tried being hurt; 'I feel so betrayed El. Can't you see that?'

She's tried bribery: 'For, let's say the next six months, you can plan the menus and I'll do the shopping. What do you say?' But all to no avail. Eleanor is determined.

'You'll have to find a new partner but I promise I won't leave Martha's Kitchen until I have found someone else to take my place. Why don't you consider the other proposal that Nigel made? Start a restaurant, with your new partner. Buy the Blue Hyacinth at Little Melding from Nigel's dad. You could ask George to lend you the money. He could afford it.'

'I couldn't ask George.'

'Why not?'

'I just couldn't.'

'You could re-mortgage the house.'

'And you imagine that Martin would agree to that!'

'Anyway, how is Martin these days? Still quiet?'

Martha sighed. 'Yes, very quiet.'

Martin knows about George. He's known since the Sunday

night Martha returned from Orford.

As she cautiously entered the front door of the house on the night of her return, Martha was hoping that her husband had gone to bed. No such luck. When she opened the door into the sitting room, she found him waiting for her on the settee.

'Where have you been?'

'Orford,' adding, as she turned back towards the door, 'And I'm exhausted after that long drive back so I think I'll. . . .'

'Orford? Orford in Suffolk?'

'Yes. And Aldeburgh. We spent a morning in Aldburgh and an afternoon at Snape.'

'We? You and Eleanor?'

'No.'

'Did Molly come down from Sheffield?' he persisted, naming an old school friend.

'I went with George.' There is a moment's silence and then Martin said very quietly, 'Do I know this . . . George?'

'You've met him at the party. George is Duncan's dad.'

'The transvestite . . . the chap who . . . .'

'Yes.'

'You spent the weekend with him?' Martin's voice was still neutral and Martha found this terrifying.

'Yes.'

'In Orford?'

'Yes and as I say: Aldeburgh and Snape.'

Very carefully, Martin folded the newspaper he hadn't been reading.

'And Minsmere. We went to Minsmere this morning.'

'How early?'

'Six.'

'You were up at six?'

'I was.'

At this point, Martin was more stunned by the fact that his wife, *his* wife, had risen from her bed on a Sunday morning to go bird watching, than he was by her infidelity. He rose to his feet.

'I'm going to bed. Switch off the lights and make sure the front door is locked. Good night.'

Since that night, Martin has said very little.

Martha broods about all of this as she puts the finishing touches to the food for the recorder orchestra's party. As far as she can gauge Martha is catering for 80 guests. Bridget, the conductor and leader of the recorder orchestra, had been vague over numbers.

'Let's see, there's roughly twenty-four players, when they all turn up, which is never, and most of them are bringing four guests, or so they say.'

Martha surveys the trays, cartons plastic containers of food spread all over the work surfaces of her kitchen and is still not entirely confident that there will be enough. She wishes that Eleanor were here to reassure her. Perhaps I should make some coleslaw she is muttering to herself when the telephone rings.

'Hello?'

'Hello, Martha.' It's Jill.

'Martha, I want you and Martin to come round to my flat for dinner tonight.'

'Sorry, but that's quite out of the question.'

'I know this is short notice, but it's really important that you both come. I spoke to Martin yesterday. He's agreed.'

'That's all very well, but he's not catering for over eighty people tomorrow night.'

'Eleanor said that you had done all the preparations.'

'So you've been talking to Eleanor as well as to Martin?'

'Yes. I've been seeing quite a lot of Eleanor but I haven't

time to go into all that now Martha.' Go into all what?

'Please say you'll come. I've cooked especially.'

'I had no idea that you cooked, Jill.'

'I didn't, but I've been having lessons and you and Martin will be my first real guests since I began to cook seriously.'

Martha doesn't know what to make of all this but she is running late and needs to wind the conversation up quickly.

'Sorry but it's not possible. On top of everything else Jeremy rang last night to say that he would be coming home for the weekend.'

'I thought he was back at college.'

'He is. He went up a fortnight ago but as usual he's left half his stuff behind and so he's coming home today to collect it and bringing his girlfriend, a music student, with him. So you can see why tonight's impossible, Jill. Now I must go because I still have to pack my boot before I go to meet their train.'

'Jeremy can take this girl out for a meal tonight. There's that new Italian place off the High Street.'

'And there's another thing. Martin and I . . . well, he's been a bit quiet lately and . . . .'

'He told me.'

'He told you what?'

'He told me about you and that transvestite. I'm disappointed in you, Martha.'

'He told you about me and George!'

'Well Eleanor told me first. I think Eleanor's disappointed as well. How could you do it Martha?'

'I really can't believe I'm hearing this. Has it slipped your mind that you had an affair with my husband? How you have the nerve to . . . .'

Martha catches sight of the kitchen clock. 'Oh god, look at the time.'

'I know you have to meet Jeremy's train so you better go.

Come round to mine about seven tonight and you can tell me off then.'

And the line goes dead.

Martha arrives at the station to meet Jeremy and Kate only to discover that the train from London is late. She is gazing at her mobile, wondering whether to ring Eleanor and find out what's going on, when it rings. It's George. Martha sighs. She really does not want to speak to George right now.

Since their weekend at Orford, George and Martha have only met twice. And it's all Martha's fault. George rang Martha every day during the week following their parting outside the Black Swan, but every time he suggested meeting, she made some excuse. In the end George's patience ran out and he threatened to come to her house and drag her out if she continued to put him off, so Martha agreed to meet. The rendezvous, at a noisy roadhouse outside Watford, wasn't a success. Martha, pleading a headache, only stayed an hour. Before she left, George extracted a promise that she would meet him in London the following weekend for a proper night out.

It was not George's fault that the second meeting was no more successful than the first. He booked a table at a swish Chinese restaurant in Soho and once they were ensconced in a secluded alcove of the restaurant, complete with marble floors, discreet lighting, white linen table cloths, red and gold dragons glaring down from the walls, George set out to amuse and entertain. Martha drank the wine, helped herself from the array of dishes that her attractive escort had ordered, smiled and nodded but George was not deceived.

'Finally he said, 'What's the matter, darling? You've not been listening to a word I've said.'

'Yes I have. You are determined to persuade Oliver to sell you this flat in Hampton Wick and the dinner party you went to last week was so boring that you nearly fell asleep into your soup.'

George smiled and embarked on a story about his managing director who had just become engaged to some starlet half his age. Martha tried to concentrate but found herself examining George's mobile lips, expensively maintained white teeth, his dark, deep-set eyes. She recalled how excited she had been when she met this man that day outside Duncan's flat. Her knees had shaken then. Why weren't they shaking now? Why was she counting the minutes until she could leave this fancy restaurant and go to the station to catch the next train home?

George brought his story to an amusing conclusion and looking at her quizzically said. 'Something's wrong. Tell me.'

'George . . . .' Martha took a deep breath. Suddenly she knew what she had to say. Suddenly it was all very simple.

'Yes, Martha?'

'It's over, George.'

For a moment, George made no reply. He poured himself another glass of wine and drank half of it. Then he topped up his glass and replenished his plate from the vast array of unfinished dishes on the table in front of him. At last he said: 'You can't expect me to finish all this.'

Martha put a spoonful of chicken and some more rice on her plate.

'Say something, George, please.'

He sighed. 'I don't know what to say to be quite honest. What else is there to say? I don't understand why, though.'

Martha sighed. 'I don't know why, myself. You're very attractive, George . . . .'

'Oh for god's sake.'

'The truth is, I can't sustain this relationship, when Martin is so quiet.'

'Sustain this relationship! Christ!'

'I don't know what he's thinking.'

'So you are dumping me because Martin's not talking to you?'

'George, I'm not the woman you thought I was. I'm not the woman I thought I was. I can't do an affair when Martin is, well, so remote. Isn't that pathetic?'

'The way you're pushing your food around the plate is pathetic. In fact I can't stand it any longer.' George beckons the waiter. He is the kind of man that never fails to catch the waiter's eye. He pays the bill and then stands up, saying, 'I'll run you to the station.'

Since that night Martha has not heard a word from George, but now he is ringing her on her mobile. She says in a small voice:

'Hello, George.' Martha's heart lurches at the sound of her ex lover's velvety voice murmuring in her ear.

'Hello, darling. Don't worry, I'm not harassing you or anything. I just thought I ought to warn you that I will be at the recorder concert tomorrow evening.'

'I don't think the recorder concert is your sort of thing, George.'

'Perhaps not, but I'm not coming for the music or for the pleasure of seeing you, my dear. I am coming because my son Duncan has asked me to.'

'Duncan's coming to the recorder concert? Does he like Baroque music?'

'No. If you told my son that Elton John was a Baroque composer, he would not raise an eyebrow. It's because of your Lucinda that Duncan is coming to the recorder concert.'

'Lucinda isn't coming to the concert. She hates recorders.'

'Well I can assure you that your daughter is coming to the concert. And there's something else I feel you should know: your daughter is playing fast and loose with my son. And it's because of your daughter's shenanigans that Duncan and I are both coming to the concert.' Martha can't help herself. She giggles.

'George, you sound as though you are in some Victorian melodrama – fast and loose indeed. Shenanigans!' George laughs.

'Be that as it may . . . .'

'Stop it, George!'

'Okay, but you must know Duncan and Lucinda have been seeing each other.'

'I know no such thing. She's said nothing to me, although since she got this new job in town, we've been out of touch. She's been staying with a friend in Finchley. It's just Martin and me at home at the moment. Are Duncan and Lucinda really an item?'

'They are when she's not seeing the other string she's got attached to her bow.'

'Off you go again.'

'I can't help it. The words keep rolling off my tongue.'

'The last I knew, Lucinda was going out with this chap with a fancy car. She seemed quite smitten. Said he was cool.'

'No one who plays the recorder is cool.'

Martha cast her mind back to the weeks following the party.

'She met him at Eleanor's party and was very keen at first but went off him when she discovered he was another 'classical music freak' as she put it.'

'Anyway, she's told my Duncan that she's going to this concert tomorrow night.'

'Why?'

'Because she promised this Jasper chap she would go.'

'Yes. Lucinda has her faults but she always keeps her promises.'

'And when the concert's over, she is going to finish with him.'

'I see, but I still don't understand why you have to go.'

'To support my son. I'm pretty sure that he is attending the concert to make sure that your daughter keeps her word.'

'Now look here, like I said, if Lucinda makes a promise, she keeps it.'

'Be that as it may, Duncan is going to be there and he requested that I go along to give him moral support. Bye.'

And before Martha can say another word the line goes dead.

This is just as well, because when Martha looks up she sees Jeremy crossing the car park towards her. A pretty, dark-haired girl is clinging to his arm. Kate is small and slightly built with blue-black curly hair that frames a delicately boned face. She has large, slanting eyes and black curving brows that might have been painted on. She is wearing khaki cut-away trousers and a cropped black leather jacket over a white turtle neck sweater.

'Hi Martha,' carols Kate as she heaves a small back-pack onto the back seat.

'Lovely to meet you at last. Your gorgeous son has landed me on you for the weekend. Please say you don't mind. He's told me that you are very busy but we won't be any trouble I promise. Jeremy can cook. '

Martha looks with surprise at her son, who has climbed into the seat beside her. He leans over and pecks her cheek.

'Hi, mum. This is Kate, as I expect you've gathered. And she can't cook.'

Kate continues a stream of inconsequential chatter as Martha exits the car park. Jeremy smiles over his shoulder fondly, 'She never stops,' he says as his girl friend pauses for breath in the middle of explaining how she and Jeremy have found a bed-sit in Camden Town, which they moved into the previous weekend.

'It's only because I'm so excited to be here. I'll calm down in a minute, you'll see.'

Martha stops at a traffic-lights.

'So you've moved out of Duncan's flat. Is he okay about that?' she asks as she pulls away.

'I don't think he's noticed that I've gone. Duncan's not able to take in anything but the most basic information these days. He's so besotted with our Lucinda that he's barely functioning. Mum, why are you going this way?'

'I want to stop at the Community Hall to drop off some stuff for tomorrow night. The boot is stacked. I thought that you two might help me unload.'

After the first batch of food for the following night's party has been unloaded at the hall, Martha leads Jeremy and Kate back to the car. As she pulls out of the car park, she continues apologetically,

'I'm afraid you two will have to fend for yourselves tonight. Dad and I have to go out.'

'You and dad are going out?'

'We're going out to dinner.'

'With Eleanor and . . .?'

'No.'

'The Greens?' Neighbours down the road.

'No.'

'Who then? Why all this secrecy?'

'There's no secrecy. As a matter of fact your father and I are having dinner with Jill.'

'Jill! Dad's . . . ex . . . secretary?'

'Yes. She rang earlier this morning. I wasn't keen on the idea, but it seems that Martin has accepted for both of us.'

Before going to collect Jeremy and Kate from the station, Martha had rung Martin at his office. His secretary put her straight through.

'Martin?'

'Yes, Martha.'

'Jill rang.'

'She told me that she was going to contact you.'

'She wants us to go to dinner tonight but you know that I've got this recorder orchestra party tomorrow night and . . . .'

'I understood that you had finished cooking for that.'

'Yes but there's always a lot of last minute . . . .'

'Jill will be very disappointed if we don't go. She's been cooking all week.'

'I didn't know that. Martin, do you want to go?'

'Yes.'

'Well, you could go on your own. Perhaps that's what she . . .'

'She's asked us both. She wants us both to go.'

'Do you want us both to go . . . together?'

'Yes, but if you have other plans . . . .'

Martha didn't know what to say. She wanted to say a lot of things, to ask a lot of questions about why Martin wanted the two of them to dine with Jill at such short notice but something about Martin's tone forbade it. Finally she said quietly, 'Okay, Martin. I'll see you there at seven.'

'Fine.' And he rang off.

EIGHTEEN

Friday morning

Eleanor is sitting at the table in Jill's kitchen, eating smoked salmon sandwiches and watching the younger woman cut a pound of stewing steak into small cubes. Jill, her white cords and granddad shirt covered by a large blue and white striped butcher's apron, finishes cutting the meat and then turns with some apprehension to a glistening chuck of kidney.

'Just cut out the white core and then dice in the same way,' instructs Eleanor.

'Do I have to?'

'Don't think about it. Just do it.'

Jill does as she is told, while Eleanor tucks into another sandwich and then starts on a plate of Caesar salad that Jill has arranged tastefully in a small wooden bowl.

'Eight out of ten for the salad. You've been a bit heavy on the anchovy in my view though the croutons are perfect. Crisp and brown.'

'Shall I serve Caesar salad tonight?'

'No and stop looking so worried. Everything is going to be fine. Martha will be astonished.'

'But will she give me the job? That's the question.'

Jill is tossing the meat cubes in seasoned flour now. When she has finished, she opens a drawer next to the stove and takes out a large frying pan. She pours oil into the pan and then begins to cook the meat cubes in batches. Jill is a very highly organised cook and there is no sign of disorder in her immaculate kitchen. It is a large bright room with daffodil yellow walls and all the latest fittings and gadgets. A large window overlooks the leafy Grantley Avenue which faces south and a Venetian blind filters the sunlight into thick slabs of gold onto the oak table, where Eleanor is finishing her lunch. Grooved and beaded oak storage units with shining brass handles line two walls of the kitchen. A state of the art cooker with a brass hood takes pride of place in their midst. Jill's aunt's Welsh dresser, gleaming with a white and gold dinner service dominates the third wall and the dining area.

Jill has spent a lot of time in her kitchen during the past month, all the time that she has not been at work in fact. The young woman has taken only two evenings off. She attended a concert in which Manfred was playing on one occasion and allowed him to take her out to dinner on the other. These two evenings are not the only ones Manfred and Jill have spent together though. The French Horn player is so besotted with his new girl friend that he has sat in on many cooking lessons and has sampled the results. What cooking lessons?

Eleanor, run off her feet, dividing her time between the shop, builders, wholesalers and Jill, has spent much of the last month teaching Jill to cook. Martha's partner was sincere when she promised that she would not quit her catering job until she found someone else to take her place but finding that replacement proved more difficult than she anticipated. Martha refused point blank to advertise so, after sounding out various acquaintances in the catering business with no success, Eleanor was at her wit's end.

During one lunch hour, just when she had given up hope of ever finding a replacement, she chanced to meet Jill sitting at a corner table in a café in the High Street.

'Mind if I join you?'

Eleanor ordered a large pizza and, as she worked her way relentlessly through it, she told Jill all about her new job and Martha's refusal to accept her resignation. Finishing off the last crumbs of the pizza, Eleanor went on to describe the restaurant she wanted Martha to buy. Then, because Jill was such a rewarding audience, she embarked on the story of Martha's affair with George. Jill was enthralled. She couldn't remember the last time she'd had such an entertaining lunch hour. After Eleanor had finished describing Martha's weekend in Orford and Martin's ominous silence, she returned to the main theme: her new job.

'The trouble is, I can't give my full attention to it until I find someone else to take my place. I promised I would not leave until I found a suitable replacement.'

'I wish I could cook,' said Jill wistfully.

'Anyone can cook,' replied Eleanor, beckoning to the waitress.

'I can't.'

'Basically, all you have to do is follow instructions. I expect you are using the wrong cook books.'

'I haven't got any cook books. When I cook I make it up as I go along. I cook by ear.'

'Then no wonder you have so many disasters.'

'Will you teach me? If you taught me to cook, I could apply for your job. I could be Martha's new partner. I've got some money that my aunt left me and I would be willing to invest it in this restaurant you talked about.'

Eleanor was dubious at first. 'I don't think I've got the time. I really should be giving all my attention to the shop.'

'How about giving me a month? You said that anyone could cook if they followed instructions. Teach me the basics.'

'The thing is Jill, that you will have to convince Martha that you will be an asset to the business.'

'I maybe a poor cook, but I have a good business head on my shoulders. I can keep accounts. I am good with suppliers. I helped my aunt run her book shop for two years before she died. It was a large shop and I did all the ordering, the auditing, built a web site and organised a postal delivery service.'

Eleanor made a quick decision.

'OK, you're on. I'll come round tonight and we'll make a start.'

And that's why Eleanor is sitting at Jill's kitchen table watching her cook the main course for this evening's meal. Since that lunch a little over a month ago, Jill has made enormous progress under Eleanor's exacting tutelage. She has learnt how to make a basic stock. She has mastered a range of sauces and can grill, sauté, roast without burning and, most importantly of all, she knows how to follow a recipe.

Jill takes the already sliced onions and fries them in oil until they are golden and transparent. Eleanor, who has finished her lunch, takes her plate over to the sink and rinses it under the tap.

'I'm going to leave you now. I promised Brian the builder I'd look in this afternoon. He said he'd have the changing rooms finished today and I want to make sure everything is going according to plan.'

Jill looks up from the pan that she is stirring. She is not happy. Eleanor pats her shoulder reassuringly: 'You'll be fine. You know what you have to do. Have you decided on the wine?'

'Martin's bringing the wine.'

'I'll look in about six to make sure everything's okay. Now stop worrying.'

'I can't help it. There's so much at stake.'

'It's only a job. You like your present job, don't you? If this fails you can just . . . .'

'It's not just about the job. What I want is to bring Martin and Martha back together again. He loves her, you know. And Martha loves him, in spite of the fact that he's tone deaf. She shouldn't have slept with that chap, George. It was wrong.'

'I don't agree but I haven't time to argue just now. I have to

178

go. Remember to leave yourself time to have a shower and a lie down.'

Friday evening
Martin Brown arrives at his ex-mistress's front door promptly at six forty-five pm. He is wearing a charcoal grey suit, a dark blue shirt and a blue and white striped tie. He is dressed formally because he has been entertaining two important clients from abroad.

Martin has taken his wife's affair very badly. He still finds it difficult to believe that she embarked on an affair with this chap George, a chap who gets himself up in women's clothes, for god's sake! A chap whose wife is having an affair with a Catholic priest, according to Jeremy. A chap who has the gall to take another chap's wife to a fucking bird sanctuary that is only a stone's throw away from where a chap is fishing.

Martin doesn't know what to do about it all and that's the truth. Eleanor seems to think that this dinner party at Jill's flat will help. Martin can't see how but he's gone along with it all the same. For the life of him he can't think of anything else to do.

Before Martin can ring Jill's doorbell, the door opens and there is Eleanor dressed in a pale blue woollen suit looking as attractive as ever. She leans towards Martin in a waft of expensive perfume, kisses him and then draws back to study him more closely:

'You've lost weight Martin and it suits you.'

Martin shuffles self-consciously and pats his stomach,

'What are you doing here?'

'I've been giving Jill a little moral support, but I'm on my way now to meet Nigel'.

'Has Martha arrived yet?'

'No, but you go on in. Jill's in the kitchen fussing over the

179

starters. I'll see you tomorrow night, I expect. Bye.'

As Martin closes the door behind him, Jill appears at the doorway to his right. She is wearing a black velvet skirt, a long sleeved silver-grey shirt with a deep cut flounced neckline and high-heeled ankle boots. Jill's cheeks are flushed, her eyes anxious.

'Martin, lovely to see you.' She leads her ex-lover into the kitchen. He takes the two wine bottles from the bag he is carrying and then goes to the fridge.

'I'll put the white in here.'

'I want to show you where everything is Martin before I go.'

'I thought you were eating with us.' Jill ignores this remark and gestures towards the stove.

'You will start with the prawn bisque.' She points to two white and gold bowls placed nearby on the work-top. 'And these are the plates you serve it in. Okay?'

She goes over to the fridge and points inside to the top shelf: 'There are the sweets and on the top shelf the cheese. Martin, are you paying attention?' She moves back to the stove.

'For the main course there is steak and kidney pudding as you see. This is the potato/parsnip gallette but be careful when you take it out because the dish is very hot. Have you got all that?' Before Martin can speak the doorbell rings.

'That will be Martha. I will let her in and then leave. Jill goes to the kitchen door and then turns to look back very earnestly at Martin.

'I just want to say two things before I go. First: Martin this is your chance to make it up with Martha. Neutral ground and all that. You love her and I'm sure that she loves you. She's not very good at showing it, that's all.'

'I'm not so sure about that.'

'And second: you'll find a note pad and pen on the table.

Please make sure that Martha marks each dish out of ten. You'll see I have listed the dishes and left space beside each for the mark.'

The door bell rings again and Jill is through the kitchen door before Martin can voice the hundred or so questions that are queuing up in his mind. He hears Jill's voice.

'Hello Martha, how lovely to see you. Are these for me? You'll find a vase in the bottom cupboard to the right of the sink. Must dash.'

'Jill!' There is a sort of wailing cry from Martha and then Martin hears the front door close.

A few seconds later, Martin's wife walks into the kitchen clutching a bunch of pink carnations to her chest. She is wearing a midnight-blue calf length skirt that flutes out from her knees, a matching short sleeved fluffy jumper and the single strand of pearls he had bought her for their fifth wedding anniversary. Her hair is loose, the way he likes it. Her face is pale and her eyes huge. She walks slowly into the room, on heels that make her almost as tall as him.

'Martin?' She says hesitatingly. 'What's happening?'

'You look lovely, Martha.'

Martha's eyes search her husband's face.

'So do you, Martin,' she says. 'I don't believe that I've seen that shirt before.'

'It's the first time I've worn it. I bought it yesterday. I haven't seen that skirt before either . . . or the top.'

'I bought them this morning.'

'The colour suits you. Shall I take the flowers?'

'I'll see to them.' She blushes and goes over to the cupboard by the sink and emerges with a cut glass vase. Martin can't remember the last time he saw his wife blush. He watches her fill the vase with water and begins to arrange the flowers. When she's finished, her eyes go to the table set for two. Then she moves round the settings, fiddling with knives, forks, glasses.

'So she's not coming back? All this is for just the two of us?'

Martin is at the stove now. He puts a low heat under the bisque and begins to stir.

'I think she's playing you at your own game.'

Martha doesn't know how to reply to this so after a pause she says, 'Jill seems to have gone to a lot of trouble.'

Martin laughs. 'She's trying to impress you.'

'In what way? Why should she want to impress me?'

'Perhaps it will become clearer as the evening goes on.' He pauses. 'If it goes on.'

Martha picks up a wine glass and then puts it down again. She folds and unfolds a napkin.

'She told me that she had been cooking for this evening all week.'

'Judging by what I've seen, I'd say she has. Everything is ready. It only requires serving up and I've been given instructions on all that.'

Martha looks up now and smiles nervously.

'Well since she's cooked, it does seem churlish not to eat. What do you think?'

'I agree. Before we start would you like a glass of white wine?'

'Please.' Martin points to the door that leads to the hall.

'Go into the hall, turn left and you will see a door ahead of you. That leads into Jill's sitting room. Make yourself comfortable. I'll bring the drinks through.'

Martha follows her husband's instructions and finds herself in a large room. Long, dark-red velvet curtains, swinging from golden rings frame the long sash windows. An expensive looking Persian carpet covers the floor. Such is the size of the room that it accommodates two other easy chairs, a deep sofa covered in a maroon velvety material, a wall of bookcases, a grand piano, a roll top desk, a television set and music centre. In front of the open fire is a dark mahogany coffee table, scattered with magazines and recorder music. Martha sits on the sofa as Martin enters the room and hands her one of two glasses that he is carrying. Then he sits down in the easy chair by the fire.

Martha decides that honesty is the best policy: 'I feel very awkward being here, Martin. You have to admit it's rather bizarre: your ex-mistress inviting us for dinner and then, well, just leaving.'

Martin relishes the sight of his wife perched on the edge of Jill's sofa taking nervous sips of wine.

'No more bizarre than you inviting her to dinner and then disappearing off the face of the earth.' Martha stiffens as Martin wriggles into a more comfortable position in his chair. She knows the signs. Her husband is about to attack.

'Since we are talking 'bizarre', wouldn't you agree that it was pretty bizarre you sending my mistress chocolates and flowers.'

'Not as bizarre as you with a stripper on your back.'

That should stop him in his tracks. But no, here he comes again: 'I think you trying to teach me to play the recorder rates pretty high in the bizarre stakes.'

He fires the decisive shot: 'Or that man dressing up in your frock and trying to seduce me. Come on, Martha. You can't get more bizarre than that.' He continues relentlessly: 'I tell a lie. The chap then goes on to seduce my wife. Now that's about as bizarre as you can get.' Set and match. And then, to her dismay, he asks bluntly: 'Is he better in bed than me, Martha?'

But Martha counters, 'Was Jill better than me?' Martha is down, but she's not out.

Martin sighs, 'Is that what your affair is all about: getting even?'

'No . . . yes . . . perhaps partly.'

There is a long silence, which Martha is the first to break: 'I don't think it's a very good idea make comparisons. I'll just say this Martin, and only this. George talked a lot . . . in bed. Too much.'

'So did Jill.'

'No!' Martha is dying to ask more but knows this would be unwise.

'She . . . gushed a lot. That's all I'm saying.'

'George was a bit too accomplished, if you must know.'

'I'm not sure that I do want to know that.'

'As if he'd had a lot of practise . . . with a lot of people. And read books about what to do.'

They both think about this quietly and then Martin says gently, 'We learnt together, if I remember rightly.'

'We did and I don't remember us referring to any books.'

'Do you recall that Sunday morning when Jeremy, who must have been about seven at the time, came in and asked if we were fighting?' Martin says thoughtfully.

'And you said we were playing.'

'And he said playing horses?'

'And you said yes.'

Martin gets up from his chair and joins his wife on the sofa. Martha is astonished to find that she is trembling. He takes one of her hands and says slowly,

'There's just two questions I want to ask you, Martha.'

'Yes, Martin?'

'The first is: shall we eat?'

'Let's.'

Martha leaps to her feet, leads the way into the kitchen and sits down at the table. As he goes over to the stove Martin says,

'There is another question. When you were talking about George just now, you used the past tense.'

'It's over.'

'Good.'

Martin pours the bisque into two white dishes, carries them to the table and sits down.

'I'm no good at affairs, Martin. I'm not the sophisticated woman of the world that I thought I was.' Then very quietly, 'Turns out I prefer what I've got. Turns out that I'm terrified of losing it.'

'Me, you mean.'

'Yes, you, Martin.'

'Well you haven't. So eat your soup.'

Martha lifts her spoon and takes a sip. Then another, then another. 'This is delicious. I had no idea that Jill could cook.'

Martin is tucking into the bisque now. He smacks his lips in appreciation.

'It's sublime.'

'What's next?' Martha has finished the bisque.

'Steak and kidney pudding.'

'My favourite. How did she know? Did you tell her?'

'No, but perhaps Eleanor did. She and Jill have been seeing quite a lot of each other lately.'

'How come?'

'How many out of ten would you give the bisque?'

Martha lays down her fork and looks in astonishment at the husband.

'What on earth are you talking about?'

Martin picks up the pen and pad that Jill has left lying on the table and hands it to Martha. She reads: 'Bisque, steak and kidney, aubergine . . . this is a menu?'

'No, a score sheet.'

'You are joking. This is bizarre Martin.'

Martin grins, 'Not as bizarre as . . . .'

'All right, all right, let's not start all that again.'

'Go on then. Mark the bisque.'

'I shall do no such thing.'

'Let me put it this way: no marks, no steak and kidney pudding.'

Martha sighs and writes.

'What did you give her?'

'Nine and a half .'

'That wasn't so difficult was it? Now pour out some more wine, while I serve up the main course.'

Martin busies himself at the stove and Martha pours the wine.

'Are you trying to get me drunk,' she says archly.

'Do I need to?' Martin places two large dinner plates and a dish of vegetables on the table.

To his astonishment and delight his wife blushes. Martin savours the moment. He should. It will be a long time before he will see his wife blush again.

Martha murmurs demurely and we all know that Martha doesn't do demure as a rule: 'No . . . but let's wait until we get home before we . . . .'

'Whatever you say, darling.'

'Darling? Darling? You never call me darling.'

'Well, darling, there's always a first time for everything.'

Midnight

A car draws up outside the flat in Grantley Avenue. Manfred is at the wheel and Jill is in the passenger seat beside him. The couple get out of the car.

'Tinky Winky, do you think they've gone?'

'Well, there's only one way to find out Lah Lah.'

Manfred unlocks the front door and the couple enter the

house. All is silence. Manfred leads the way out of the hall and then into the kitchen. He switches on the light. The room is pristine. The dishwasher is still humming away though and when Jill opens the fridge door she can see a number of plastic containers arranged tidily on the shelves. Then Manfred spots an envelope propped up against the vase of carnations on the dining table. He hands it to Jill. She opens it and reads out loud, 'Thanks for a wonderful meal. We both really enjoyed it. See you tomorrow, love, Martha and Martin.'

Jill looks anxiously at Manfred. 'What do you think that means Tink?'

Manfred moves swiftly to Jill's side. He kisses her gently on the lips.

Jill scans the table: 'Martha hasn't left the mark sheet.'

Manfred slides his hands beneath Jill's silk shirt. 'Let's go to bed. It's late.'

Jill nuzzles her face against his chin, which is brave, since Manfred is one of those men who should shave twice a day. And he hasn't.

'Do you think I've got the job, Tink?'

Without replying, Manfred takes the young woman's hand and leads her out of the kitchen, across the hall and into her bedroom. Expertly he manoeuvres her onto the bed.

'Shall I ring Martha and ask, Tinky?' Then he stands and unzips his trousers. Jill smiles and says, 'I take it that's a no,' and wriggles round to undo her skirt.

'Let me. You can't ring Martha at this time, Lah Lah. She and Martin will be in bed. And you wouldn't want to interrupt anything would you?'

Jill giggles. 'You are clever Tinky. I would never have thought of that.'

Manfred lowers his eyes in mock modesty: 'Tell me what to do now, Lah.'

'You could take my shirt off, Tinks.'

'Would you like that, Lah?'

Slowly, Manfred undoes the buttons on the front of Jill's silk shirt and slides it down from her shoulders. Then he reaches round to undo her bra.

'And this?'

'Please, Tinks.'

'What shall I do now, Lah?'

'I just can't think, Tinks. Got any ideas?'

'One or two.'

Manfred is right. Martha and Martin are in bed. Martin has his arm around his wife. Her head is resting on his chest.

'How was it for you, Martha?'

'Lovely, tiger.'

'How many out of ten?'

Martha raises herself onto one elbow and looks searchingly into her husband's face. Unfortunately, it is unreadable. An oriental could take lessons in inscrutability from Martin Brown. Finally she says, 'You shouldn't ask questions like that.'

'Why?' While she is still marshalling her thoughts, he continues, 'The question still stands. Have you got a problem with it?'

'OK. Nine and a half.'

'What do I have to do to get the other half.'

Martha thinks for a moment and then says:

'Do it again . . . now.'

'Nine and half it is then.'

Saturday morning

It is nine fifteen on a bright autumn morning. Martha, who is standing at her stove frying bacon and eggs, glances out of her kitchen window and sees that the leaves on the trees in the garden have turned to gold. She is humming softly to herself as she turns the bacon. Martin enters the kitchen so quietly that his wife is unaware of his presence until he kisses her gently on the back of the neck. She smiles and allows his arms to encircle her for a moment. As she turns back to the stove, she says indulgently, 'You are looking very pleased with yourself this morning.

Martin seats himself at the kitchen table. Martha has laid places for four, together with a jug of orange juice, a basket of warm rolls and a pot of coffee.

'I can't remember the last time we had bacon and eggs for breakfast.'

'I thought you might need the extra protein,' she says as she takes a tray of mushroom and tomatoes from under the grill and then serves them out together with the bacon and eggs. The couple tuck into their breakfast in companionable silence until Martha murmurs innocently, 'Sleep well?'

'Like a log. Full of beans this morning,' stuffing a forkful of bacon and mushrooms into his mouth.

'I noticed.'

'Did I earn the extra point?'

Before she can reply, the kitchen door opens and Eleanor enters the room. She takes in the scene of domestic bliss in front of her and grins.

'All went well last night then, I see?'

Martha puts down her knife and fork: 'My, you're a sly one. She's your replacement, I suppose.'

'Aren't I just? And yes.' Smugly, Eleanor sits down at the table and helps herself to a glass of orange juice.

'Did you enjoy the meal?' she says with a dirty grin.

Martha says primly, 'The steak and kidney pie was a master stroke. I expect that was your idea.'

'Might have been, but Jill has worked very hard this last

month and I think that meal proves that she has the makings of a good cook. I hope you gave her full marks and my job.'

'The job's hers. Jill scored very high on the whole.'

'What didn't she score high on?'

'Well, I thought the side dishes to the steak and kidney pie were a bit pretentious.'

Eleanor groans. 'I told her not to serve the spicy grilled aubergine. You must have given her full marks for the puddings though.'

'We didn't try any of the puddings in the end, did we Martin?'

He reaches for the coffee pot and says, 'No, by pudding time we had other things on our minds.'

'I hope you didn't get to grips with the other things on your minds all over Jill's sofa. She's just had those covers cleaned and if you're leaving that bacon, Martha . . . thanks, and the crusty roll? Great. I didn't have time for a proper breakfast this morning.'

'Everything ready for tonight?' says Martin, pouring Eleanor a cup of coffee.

'Just about. Jeremy and Kate helped me transport the food yesterday.'

'So I might be able to fit in a round of golf then.' He turns to Eleanor, who is buttering her third roll.

'Do you think Nigel would fancy joining me?'

'I'll ask him.'

Martha drains her coffee and then says hesitantly,

'There's just one thing I ought to mention about tonight, Martin.'

'And what's that, my dove?'

'George is coming . . . to the concert.'

'George?' he asks quietly, from behind the newspaper.

'George. You know, Duncan's dad.'

NINETEEN

Saturday afternoon

The final rehearsal of the recorder orchestra is not going well.

'Kylie, wake up. If you cast your eye in this direction every now and again you wouldn't be a bar behind. Norman, you are lagging as well and you missed the key change after the double bar. Get a grip both of you.'

Jill gives a sympathetic smile to the ex-flasher but gets a stony stare in return.

'You are taking it too fast,' says Kylie in the voice of a petulant child. The other two descant players put down their instruments in a gesture of solidarity.

'She's right.' says Mavis. 'You have to slow down.' And she folds her arms across her flat chest as Brenda snaps, 'All you do is wave your arms about. We have to play the notes you know.'

This is mutiny. Luke glances nervously at his leader. Bridget is famous for her fiery temper and she is winding herself up for a major tantrum any minute now. He decides to intervene.

'Let's take five. Or better still, let's take ten.'

At this point, everyone begins to shout at once, but Felix with his colonel of the regiment voice, overrides them all.

'There's trouble in the ranks, Bridget, and a good officer knows when his men have had enough. Tell them to stand down for ten minutes, there's a good chap.'

The conductor knows when she is beaten. Felix does not often speak out but when he does, it is best to pay attention.

'Oh very well.'

There is a reason behind all this ill-temper. When the players assembled for rehearsal that afternoon, they found that it was already underway. Four string players, who no one even recognised, were rehearsing the Samartini recorder concerto with Jasper, who was playing the solo. As the players shuffled to their places he was storming into the last thirty-two bars.

'Well done, Jasper,' cried Bridget as he finished.

'Bravo,' shouted the fat, bearded man, in his middle fifties, who was leading the quartet. Playing second violin was an emaciated dark-haired child, his fifteen-year-old daughter, Daisy. On viola was a round-shouldered, aesthetic looking man and on cello a Titian-haired beauty who tossed her head a lot.

'Brilliant, darling,' she gushed in a throbbing contralto.

Jasper, resuming his usual seat among the other players, tried and failed to look suitably modest as the conductor turned to the other players and said, 'Surprise, everyone. Meet the Stenor String quartet. This is Brian,' pointing to the bearded leader, 'and his talented daughter, Daisy. Then there's Brendan on viola and Noreen on cello.' The members of the quartet beamed at the recorder players and the players glared sullenly back.

'But I thought Norman was playing the Samartini,' said Luke. 'And I can't remember you saying anything about a string quartet performing tonight or did I miss something?'

'They will be playing in just a couple of pieces and as for the Samartini, nothing was cast in stone.'

'Yes, but Norman always . . . .'

'We need Norman on bass.'

Nothing more was said but no one was happy, especially Norman. The Samartini was his special party piece. No wonder he was sulking behind his contra.

So the rehearsal got off to a bad start and went from bad to worse as the afternoon progressed.

She started on the descants first: 'Descants, you are too loud. Tongue more gently. You are all playing sharp. It wouldn't be so bad if you were in tune with each other, but you are not.'

Then she began picking on other players: 'Norman you were all over the place at bar 40 or was it 43. Faith, you came in a bar early at C. Melody, oh all right, Shaz, you played through all the rests in the final eight. We'll have to run through it again, from the top.'

Soon after that, Luke suggested a break and the members of the orchestra had a chance to vent their spleen as their conductor went outside for a quick fag.

'The woman's off her trolley. No one could be expected to play at that speed.'

'She thinks she's Simon Rattle.'

'I was not sharp. I never play sharp. I've got perfect pitch, or as good as.'

'My headache's come on again. I need a lie down.'

'Inviting that quartet without so much as a by your leave.'

'I'm off,' says Shaz putting on her leather jacket. 'I never wanted to play in this fuckin' concert anyway.'

Jill rises to the occasion like the trouper she is.

'I'll go wrong if you don't play, Shaz. You know I rely on you to keep me in the right place.'

Shaz unzips her jacket, 'You don't always count the rests. That's why you get lost.'

'I know. That's why I need you.' Mollified, Shaz sits down again.

'All right but someone 'as to tell 'er.'

When Bridget returns to the hall finally, her face has resumed its normal colour. She takes her place on the rostrum.

'All right, everyone, let's go.'

'Just one thing Bridget,' says Luke, 'before we start.'

The conductor raises her eyebrows: 'Well?'

'Sorry, but I can't manage the Bransles at the new speed.'

'I find that difficult to believe, Luke.'

'Neither can I,' says Mavis.

'Can't be done, my dear,' from Felix.

Bridget opens her mouth and then closes it again. For once common sense prevails. 'Okay,' she says and then hums the top line of the piece at a slower tempo. She looks round at the assembled players. 'Is that all right?'

They nod. She lifts her baton and they begin.

At letter A, Luke, who is playing second tenor, glances across at Norman. The elderly man catches the social worker's eye and winks. For some reason, and he can't put his finger on why, Luke is uneasy.

A bad rehearsal makes a good performance, or so the saying goes. Perhaps that's right because half an hour into the evening concert, every seat in the house is filled and the recorder orchestra is playing well. Not everyone is enjoying the music though. Sandwiched between Duncan and his dad, Lucinda is compelled to watch the man who had forced her to sit through three chamber and two madrigal concerts, playing solo squeaky. Even George enjoys the performance of whatever-it-was. 'Bravo!' He shouts. It seems that they are everywhere, these music geeks. Just like rats, there is always one at least three feet from where you are sitting.

After the Samartini concerto, Lucinda shuts down and tunes out. The trouble is that as soon as she switches off the music, her present problem: how to make sure she dumps that self-satisfied creep before he dumps her first, elbows itself into the forefront of her mind.

When Lucinda first laid her plans for the evening of the concert, the sequence of events seemed straightforward enough. She would dress to kill, so that Jasper could see what he would be missing, make sure she arrived before the whole thing began, tell him he was history and then make a rapid exit. She had promised Jasper that she would come to the concert and she would keep her promise. She hadn't said that she would stay and listen to it though had she?

Unfortunately, Lucinda did not explain this scenario to Duncan. This was a mistake. For reasons that he failed to explain, Duncan insisted on attending the concert himself and then made matters worse by inviting his father along. Since Duncan and his dad were coming to the concert she would be obliged to stay and, well, listen.

The first part was easy though. Lucinda swept her newly-highlighted hair into a French pleat, applied her make-up with especial care and then donned the smart black matador pants with matching jacket, which she had found in a boutique off Bond Street.

During the course of the journey to the concert in George's BMW, Lucinda forgot that she had been annoyed with Duncan for bringing his father along. This was because George set out to charm. He complimented the young woman on her appearance, showed a flattering interest in her new job and then kept her amused with a stream of self-depreciating anecdotes. Sitting in the front passenger seat, Lucinda was blithely unaware that she was making eyes at her mother's ex lover.

When the trio arrived outside the concert venue, Lucinda parted from the two men.

'See you in a bit,' she said. 'I'm going back stage to find Jasper.'

And was rewarded by, 'That's my girl,' from Duncan's father. 'If it were done, then 'twere well it were done quickly.'

When she opened the street door of the institutional looking red brick building where the concert was to be held, Lucinda found herself in an equally institutional foyer. Notices about local events covered the walls and in the centre was a table piled high with programmes behind which two very plain women were seated. The door leading into the main hall was ajar and through it the girl could hear the sound of music and voices.

Peering through the door she saw rows of black chairs laid out in two ranks and beyond, a sort of platform on which were arranged two semi-circles of stands. Talking quietly amongst themselves, a few of the players were already seated at some of the stands. Others were gathered behind the platform.

As she hesitated by the door, Lucinda saw a dark-haired woman, carrying a sheaf of papers, push her way through the standing players. The music that she could hear was coming from two people who were seated at stands, placed next to and below the platform. One of the musicians was a red-headed girl, wearing a long black skirt and a green flounced blouse, cut so low that, as she bent forward to play her cello, it revealed most of her large breasts. The other was Jasper. As he played, his eyes went back time and again to those quivering mounds of flesh. Lucinda knew that expression. She had seen it on Jasper's face the night of Eleanor's party. Only then he was looking at her. What Lucinda did not know was that Jasper fell in love on an average of once a month and that her month was up.

As she hesitated, wondering whether to march over to the players and say her piece, the music stopped. Good, now was her chance. Unfortunately, at this point a bald-headed man sitting behind a very large instrument – she didn't know recorders grew to that size – caught her eye. There was something vaguely malevolent about the man. He was just sitting there, fixing the two performers with a basilisk stare.

Lucinda took a couple of steps into the hall but almost immediately was stopped in her tracks once again. This was because once the impromptu 'recital' had finished all the other members of the orchestra began to play at once. Lucinda did not know it but the players were practising all the tricky bits in the forthcoming concert. The problem was that each individual player was practising a different 'tricky bit'. All Lucinda heard, of course, was a cacophony of dissonant sounds, mainly at the top end of the human hearing range, the range that sets your teeth on edge.

Seeking distraction from the racket, she allowed her eyes to wander over the perpetrators. Unfortunately the first player on whom her eyes alighted was Jill, the bitch who had seduced her father. Then she saw someone else that she sort of recognised. What was his name? Luke. Ah yes, Eleanor's ex. And then she noticed that Jasper had moved up onto the platform and was sitting down next to a middle-aged man with a straggling grey beard. Jasper wasn't talking to the man though. How could he when that top-heavy cellist had followed and was lolling all over him? She was leaning over so far that there was a serious danger that Jasper's head would get jammed between her breasts. Disgusted, Lucinda turned away. Then, with a start she remembered that she was there to tell that self-satisfied creep that he was dumped. But how could she tell him when the blob of lard was practically sitting on his face?

Suddenly it was too late. Some old biddy selling tickets was asking Lucinda if she had one. More and more people were arriving now and just as Lucinda was wondering whether to go back into the concert hall again, Manfred materialised at her elbow. Behind him loomed a very tall, thin man wearing dark glasses. Before Lucinda could move away Manfred insisted on introducing his companion:

'This is Falcon, Lucinda, a trumpet player friend of mine.' Did he say Falcon?

The thin man leered, revealing a row of nicotine stained teeth. 'So this is the famous Lucinda. I'm surprised old Manfred allowed you to escape.'

Lucinda ignored the man. 'What are you doing at a recorder concert, Manfred?' She asked faintly.

'I've come to support Jill.'

'Jill?' He can't mean Jill, not that Jill.

'We're together.'

Lucinda decided that she must be hearing things. Was this the onset of early Altzeimer's disease or possibly a brain tumour? Then, to her relief George and Duncan were by her side.

'Did you do the dread deed?' Asked George. Lucinda shook her head.

'Never mind. There's always the interval,' he reassured her as she guided the two men to their seats.

So I will have to speak to Jasper at the interval, Lucinda tells herself as the players swing into a lively march. The new piece sets George's foot tapping. She turns her head and finds herself gazing into a pair of dark-brown eyes that seem to search into the deepest recesses of her soul.

'You don't look like your mother, Lucinda,' he murmurs.

'But you don't know her very well, do you?'

'I wouldn't say that,' says George and turns away.

George's foot is not the only one that is tapping. Sitting in the row in front are a number of rugby players and their wives, press-ganged into attending the concert by Nigel.

'Oh come on. It's only for an hour or so. Then we can go to the pub. Okay, the first two shouts are mine.'

He called in a favour as well: 'You owe me. Who got you to your wedding in one piece? Who unchained you from that lamp post?

The rugby crowd has not enjoyed the concert so far. They are not into baroque music. Scrum Half has spent half the time looking at his watch to make sure that it hasn't stopped and the other half trying to get a better view of that sexy cellist's boobs. Everyone perks up a notch when the recorder orchestra swings into the Sousa march, though.

The row in front of the rugby crowd is entirely taken up by friends of Luke: the Morris Men, their wives and families. They enjoy the march. A couple of them begin to whistle along. Bridget's mother, who is sitting on the front row, turns round and gives them one of her famous stares. She is a retired headmistress so it is a formidable stare but the two Morris Men have been stared at before so they are not intimidated. Soon the whole team, together with their wives and families are whistling or humming along with the orchestra. Of course, the rugby contingent join in and gather up George, along with the entire back row, except Lucinda, who also begin to clap. Martin, sitting on the front row with Jeremy and Kate to his left and Martha to his right brings in the other half of the audience and then everyone in the hall, well, nearly everyone, is clapping, whistling and singing along. Bridget is delighted and turns round to conduct.

There's a lot of noise in the hall now, but not enough to awaken Frank, Miriam's husband, who is sitting next to Bridget's aunt on the front row. Frank managed to drop off even before Jasper had finished playing his solo and Beryl, Felix's wife, sitting next to him, resplendent in a wide brimmed blue hat, is too affronted to wake him up. She is counting the minutes until this ghastly affair is over and hopes none of her bridge playing friends get to hear where she spent Saturday evening.

Elated by the triumph of the Sousa march the members of the orchestra, and string quartet, stream out to meet their friends during the interval. Bridget is flushed with success. She got a real buzz out of conducting the entire audience. Norman, who is still seated at his stand watches her sourly as she trips down the aisle to greet her admirers.

She beams at her mother and kisses her aunt, 'Just like the last night of the proms don't you think? For our next concert, I think I'll find an arrangement for recorders of Land of Hope and Glory.'

Eleanor has spotted Luke chatting to two of the Morris Men. She picks her way through the crowd and, seeing her approach, Luke crosses the hall to meet her.

'You look lovely, El,' he says wistfully. Wearing a short red, woollen dress, matching shoes, lipstick and ear-rings, long loops of brightly coloured beads that swing to her shoulders, she does. She kisses his cheek.

'Jill looks lovely too,' Eleanor whispers.

Surprised, Luke glances across the room to where Jill, clad in a long dark green skirt and sleeveless lemon top, is chatting to Manfred and a chap who looks like he's a member of the Cosa Nostra.

'You and Jill have a lot in common,' continues Eleanor, who has decided that Martha isn't the only one who can try her hand at match making.

'You both love music and play the recorder. She adores country dancing and was quite besotted by your Morris Men. And she can cook. Did she tell you that she's going into partnership with Martha? Why don't you ask her out?'

Lucinda, George and Duncan are chatting to Jeremy and Kate. Kate is doing most of the talking;

'And me and Eleanor put up the streamers, arranged the flowers and laid the tables. Martha has these lovely blue tablecloths, a deep hyacinth colour. I must remember to ask where she bought them. Martha and Jill, in between rehearsing, put out the food. Martha's worried that the quiches will dry out but I think they will be all right. We've covered everything with cling-film. There's this marvellous pecan pie. Make sure you get a bit before it all goes. And I can't tell you how many salads . . . .'

Duncan isn't listening. He is watching Lucinda, who is watching Jasper, who is standing a few feet away, with one arm round a red-head. Jasper and the red-head are deep in conversation with a bearded man. Duncan knows that Lucinda still hasn't found an opportunity to speak to Jasper. What he doesn't know is that she's not sure that she can get up the nerve to dump Jasper now. Apart from a casual wave, Jasper has ignored Lucinda all evening. How can you dump someone who seems to have forgotten that you exist?

George, although he thinks that Kate is enchanting, isn't listening either. He is trying to locate the whereabouts of Martha. Suddenly he spots her, entering the hall through a door behind the platform. George would like to cross the room and speak to Martha only he can't because Martin has stationed himself by the door. As his wife comes into the hall, Martin catches her in his arms and kisses her. She smiles and kisses him back. George sighs. Where did he go wrong?

The interval is over. At a signal from Bridget the players begin to drift back to their stands. As he sits down in front of his, Luke notices that Norman has moved. His client has taken Colin's place and is sitting next to Jasper on the front row. What's going on? There's no time for Luke to find out though, because Kylie, Jill and Jim, three of the four soloists in the Brandenburg concerto, are taking their places in front of the orchestra. Luke, the fourth soloist, has no alternative but to take his place beside them.

There are only two items in the second half of the concert: The Brandenburg concerto and the Capriol Suite. Bridget, standing on the rostrum ready to start, beams at her players.

'A triumph,' she whispers. 'Only two more items to go and

then it's drinks all round.'

Bridget's very confident, Norman muses to himself, as he watches his leader through half closed eyes. She thinks this concert's in the bag. Well, someone ought to tell Mary Poppins up there that it's always a mistake to count your chickens before they're hatched. The concert isn't over yet. Not by a long chalk.

The Brandenburg concerto goes very well. When it's all over, a little surprised, the four soloists acknowledge the wild applause. It is the rugby crowd that lead the clapping and whistling. The fellas have enjoyed the Brandenburg. The music wasn't bad but what was particularly delectable, especially to chaps with imagination, was the sight of two very pretty girls with pipes in their mouths, swaying sexily in time to the music. Then, as if that wasn't enough there was that cellist, who every time she bent forward, showed those spectacular knockers.

The rugby crowd whistle and stamp for so long that that the four soloists come forward time and time again to take their bows. Then Bridget takes a bow herself. The applause dies down at this point but it has gone on long enough to strengthen Norman's determination to wipe the smile from Bridget's face. Soon it will be Norman's turn to smile. Soon every eye in the hall will be on him. Not yet, though. Norman is biding his time.

Martha, Kate and Eleanor listen to the first four dances in the Capriol Suite but leave the hall after the Bransles. Cakes need to be decanted from tins and arranged on plates. Salad dressings have to be applied, plates and cutlery set out. Bridget pauses long enough for the three women to slip out through the door to the rear of the orchestra and then raises her baton to begin number five. As the three women do all the things that can only be done at the last minute, the strains of Mattachins floats through to where they are working.

'Bridget's taking it at a fair lick,' comments Martha, removing the foil from the last of her special trifles. Then, standing back to look at the tables groaning under the food that she has so painstakingly prepared: 'I hope there will be enough.'

'Too late to worry about that now,' says Eleanor briskly. 'Anyway you always worry whether you've done enough.'

'And you always say it's too late to worry now.'

Martha cocks her head: 'They're into the final eight. Let's go in and watch Bridget acknowledge the applause.'

She links one arm with Eleanor and the other with Kate.

Only, as it turns out, just as Bridget is about to savour her moment of glory, Norman steals it from her. No one can fault his timing. Norman counts meticulously through the last four bars and then on the final chord he unzips and gets it out. If anything, he's slightly ahead of the beat!

Norman's moment of glory does not last long. And he is not the cynosure of all eyes, as he had hoped. This is because, in spite of the stage blocks, the players are not raised high enough for everyone in the audience to see. Norman is flashing mainly for Bridget's benefit and she sees all right. She takes one horrified look, all the colour draining from her face, gasping, 'Norman! Oh my god!' and stumbles from the rostrum as she flees the stage.

All the players, with the exception of Colin and Verity who are sitting behind the contra player, have ringside seats, of course.

Shaz cries, 'To think I was off 'ome. To think I might 'ave missed it.'

Martin and Jeremy, sitting opposite Norman on the front row, have 'grand-stand' seats as well.

'Jesus!' says Martin.

'Hung like a donkey,' says Jeremy .

The rest of the front row also has an uninterrupted view.

The reactions are variable. Bridget's mother is working herself up into a major fit of hysterics until Aunt Renie puts a stop to it.

'Pull yourself together, Joyce. You must have seen one before.' Aunt Renie is wrong. Bridget's mum has never, in spite of her three children, had such a clear few of the male organ before. It had been her policy to keep her eyes firmly closed.

Most of the second row, including Manfred and Falcon, get a good view as well. This rousing finish to an otherwise tedious concert delights Manfred's friend.

'And to think you had to persuade me to come. I can't wait to tell the rest of the section.'

Manfred looks anxiously in the direction of Jill, hoping that she has averted her eyes. She has not. His girl friend is gazing directly at Norman and she is laughing. Then she turns her eyes in his direction. The smile fades from her face. Tinky Winky is praying that Lah Lah is not making comparisons.

George, although he's on the back row, sees what has happened because he has an end seat and a clear view right along the central the aisle.

'Don't miss this, Duncan,' he calls across Lucinda. 'Contra's got his tackle out.

'Disgusting,' says Lucinda but she stands up to take a look all the same.

As soon as they hear George's words, the rugby crowd rise to their feet, whistling and cheering. One of them rushes forward with his mobile, determined to capture the moment on film. Scrum half begins to chant, 'DOGGA, DOGGA, DOGGA, DOGGA, OGGA, OGGA, GRUNGE!'

Martha, Kate and Eleanor miss 'Norman's flash.' They hear the final chord, the silence that follows and then, just as they enter the hall, Bridget rushes past them in floods of tears. What with one thing and another, by the time the three women push their way through the crowd, Luke and Jasper are standing in front of Norman and it is all over bar the shouting.

After a lot of discussion among the players it is decided that the party should continue as planned.

'Bridget's sitting in her car in pieces. How can we go ahead?'

'The party was her idea after all.'

'You went a dotted minim too far, Norman.'

'The cow had it coming.'

'Everyone is still milling about in the hall. I told my crowd there was a party after the concert.'

'That's the only reason my boyfriend agreed to come.'

'I mean there's all this food laid out.'

'I don't know what you're all arguing about. 'Course we go ahead.'

'Perhaps someone should go out and ask Bridget if she minds.'

'You go Jasper, darling. She'll listen to you.'

'Keep your nose out of this or I'll stick a pin in your fuckin' implants.'

'Shall I tell them to come in?'

'Why not?'

'It would be a pity to see it go to waste.'

Needless to say, Bridget does not attend the party and neither does her mother. Auntie Renie would have loved to stay, but in the end decided that family solidarity is more important.

The party is a huge success. Norman really enjoys himself. He's quite the hero of the hour. After a few glasses of wine, everyone there is convinced that they witnessed the 'flash.' Apart from Martha, Kate and Eleanor that is.

'I can't believe I missed it,' wails Martha.

'Thank goodness, you did,' says Martin, who does not leave her side until the end of the evening. That George chap is lurking about and you can't be too careful.

'Why? Do you imagine I'd have turned into a pillar of salt?'

'There's that, of course, but the main reason is because you'd never guess from looking at him now, but old Norman is seriously built. You might have decided that I'm selling you short.'

George enjoys the party too. He flirts with every pretty woman in the room. Lucinda, who had imagined that he had fallen for her, watches him with a mixture of disappointment and indignation. She never gets round to dumping Jasper. At about eleven thirty she wanders out into the car park for a cool off and sees Noreen climbing into her ex-boyfriend's flash car.

George does manage to catch a quick word with Martha sometime around midnight. This is because Martin relaxes his guard when he discovers that Colin, one of the players, is another computer buff. George spots Martin and his new friend deep in technicalities, in a corner of the main hall, so he makes his way to where Martha is clearing one of the tables in the room adjacent to the hall.

'An evening of surprises,' he murmurs in her ear.

Martha turns to find herself gazing into the eyes of her ex-lover. 'Hello George,' she says, wishing that he was not so attractive. 'Have you come to say goodbye?'

'Not necessarily.' He leans forward and tucks a curl behind her left ear.

'Now George. Martin and I are back together and . . . .'

'Well Duncan is talking of popping the question to your Lucinda. If she says yes, then I'll sort of be a member of the family won't I? We'll have to meet, if only at the wedding.'

Martha takes a deep breath. She must stand firm.

'That's a lot of "ifs", George and anyway, if she does say

yes and they do marry, I know you are too much of a gentleman to take advantage.'

George smiles and winks: 'I wouldn't bank on that, my dear.'